# SUNDOWN OVER
# THE SIERRAS

When Marshal Chase Farlow responds to a break-in at Macy's gun shop, he has no inkling of the ignominy it will unleash. His unfortunate shooting of the culprit forces him to leave town in disgrace. It matters not that the injury is superficial, and Farlow was only doing his duty — the boy in question is Mayor Abner Stanton's son, and the highly principled lawman has become a thorn in Stanton's side. Can Farlow somehow resurrect his tarnished reputation?

DALE GRAHAM

# SUNDOWN OVER THE SIERRAS

*Complete and Unabridged*

**LINFORD**
*Leicester*

First published in Great Britain in 2015 by
Robert Hale Limited
London

First Linford Edition
published 2016
by arrangement with
Robert Hale
an imprint of The Crowood Press
Wiltshire

A catalogue record for this book is available
from the British Library.

ISBN 978–1–4448–3042–2

Published by
F. A. Thorpe (Publishing)
Anstey, Leicestershire

Set by Words & Graphics Ltd.
Anstey, Leicestershire
Printed and bound in Great Britain by
T. J. International Ltd., Padstow, Cornwall

This book is printed on acid-free paper

# 1

## COSTLY MISTAKE

Figures were not Chase Farlow's strong point. He scratched his mat of iron-grey hair. More from frustration than anything else. His brow creased in a morose frown as straining eyes battled to make sense of the ink-penned columns. Removing a pair of wire-framed spectacles, he cleaned the lens with his bandanna. It was now well past the time he would normally have retired to his quarters above the office. Irritably he struck a match and applied it to the oil lamp.

A heavy sigh of frustration hissed from between gritted teeth as he resumed the onerous task. Juggling the monthly accounts of rentals paid by the businesses in the town of Quemado, New Mexico, was a necessary chore in order to secure his ten per cent rake-off. The cut allowed by the town council effectively brought his rather parsimonious marshal's salary up to an acceptable level.

Nevertheless it was not a job to be relished. And Chase always delayed it until the last minute. The mayor frequently had to press him at least three times before the finished books were presented for auditing. On this occasion the credit and debit columns just refused to balance. Squinting eyes sullenly surveyed the columns of scrawled writing. He felt like screwing the whole darned lot up and quitting. This was not the reason he had become a lawman.

Reaching hands were all set to rip the lot to shreds when an auspicious interruption stayed the reckless deed.

Micah Clarke who ran the livery stable at the west end of town came bustling through the door without knocking. The ostler's unexpected entry brought a welcome return of sanity to the frustrated town marshal. Although Clarke's sudden panic-stricken appearance clearly heralded trouble, Chase did not mind. This was what he had signed up for.

The old dude was panting hard, clearly having run down the street. Not an advisable way for a guy on the wrong side of sixty to get around.

'Take it easy, old-timer,' Chase advised, leaping to his feet and ushering the grizzly veteran to a seat. 'Something mighty important must be bugging you.'

The ostler indicated that a snort of whiskey was required to bring his pounding ticker back into line. Chase obliged. The hard liquor disappeared in a single gulp. Then Clarke pointed to the outside.

'Somebody is after robbing Macy's,' he blurted out. 'I just heard breaking glass coming from the rear of the gun shop. Must be some ne'er-do-wells after those new cartridge revolvers.'

Such was the popularity of the Colt

.45 among law officers, that the fabled gun had now gone into full production for general usage. Judd Macy had been quick to order in a stock. They had soon disappeared into gun belts. The third such order in the last six months was now gracing his shelves. Old cap and ball repeaters such as the famed .36 Navy Colt lay idly gathering dust.

Chase had quickly abandoned his old army Remington in favour of the new hand gun. It was far more reliable, accurate and the unique design fitted a man's hand like a second skin. No gun had previously come close to emulating the fabled 'Peacemaker'. He quickly strapped on the well-worn rig.

'You keep well out the way, Micah,' he ordered, pushing past the ostler. 'There could be lead flying around if'n these jaspers play dirty.'

Before leaving the office, he selected the appropriate key to allow entry through the front door. Only those premises considered at risk from robbery were obliged to leave a spare key with the marshal. Along with the gun store, Harvey's the jeweller, the assay office and the bank were likely to draw unwelcome attention from bandits.

Chase hurried across the street and peered through the front window. The inner sanctum of the gun store was muffled in gloom. His own hogleg firmly palmed, he gingerly unlocked the front door and entered. A shuffling at the rear indicated that old Micah had not been mistaken. Somebody had indeed broken in. And for what other purpose than to steal the latest firearms and ammunition?

'Come out where I can see you,' he called gruffly. 'Best give up now while you're able. There's no escape and my gun hand is filled and ready.'

More scrambling as the intruder made a dash for the rear door. He tripped over a box, then stumbled to his feet, ignoring a second more strident call to surrender. An early streak of moonlight slanted through the front window, revealing a shadowy form.

Chase wasted no more time on warnings. He hauled back on the trigger and sent a couple of shots towards the fleeing thief. A cry told him that the guy had been hit. Still wary — a wounded critter is always the most dangerous — he advanced carefully towards the groaning figure lying on the floor. Then another squeal of terror broke out from the back room. There were two of them. The second villain had clearly had enough. A plea for mercy was blurted out.

'Don't shoot, I'm coming out.'

The high-pitched yowl of submission came as a shock to Chase Farlow. That was no surly drawl from some hard-nosed tough on the prod. But still he maintained that innate caution that had stood him in good stead all these years hunting down brigands and outlaws.

'Come out now where I can see you,' he snarled back. 'And shuck your hardware real careful like.'

'I ain't armed, Marshal, neither of us

are,' replied the sobbing voice.

Chase ignited a lamp and held it high above his head. Yellow light flooded the room, revealing all manner of shooting accoutrements. But it was what he observed lying on the floor that brought a lump to his throat. His mouth hung open.

The wounded intruder was nought but a kid.

His buddy appeared through the rear door. This one was even younger. Hands raised, the kid was shaking with fear. A choking gurgle stuck in his throat when he saw his friend splayed out on the floor, blood soaking through the torn shirt. Another pained croak burbled forth when his bulging eyes fixed on to the loaded gun pointing his way.

'P-please don't shoot, Marshal,' stuttered the terrified youngster. 'We were only after those toy guns that Macy has on display. We didn't mean no harm.'

Chase was lost for words. He had shot down a young kid for trying to steal . . . a toy? And the victim was not just any street urchin. It was Billy Stanton lying in a pool of his own blood — the mayor's ten-year-old son.

'Go get the doc,' Chase mumbled at the other boy. Joey Wells just stood there, mesmerized, stunned into a terrified stupor. 'Hurry it up, kid!' Chase snapped out. 'Your pal is bleeding bad. He could die.'

The stern rebuke jerked the trembling boy out of his reverie. He stumbled through the front door, more than eager to quit the horrifying scene. It was all right reading about gunfights in comics. But the truth bore no relation to dime fiction. The brutal reality of life on the frontier had been brought home to him in no uncertain manner.

A closer examination of the wounded boy educed some consolation to the shocked lawman. At least it was only a superficial injury. The kid would live and be up and about within days.

And so it proved. By the end of the

week, Billy Stanton was bragging to all his friends about the exploit. The break-in was considerably embellished to make him out to be a hero. The same could not be said for Marshal Chase Farlow, who was summoned before the town council to answer for his ignoble deed.

As he waited nervously in the room outside the council chamber, his thoughts flashed back over how his life had been brought to this lugubrious state.

It was like when he had sat outside the teacher's study as a kid himself, waiting to receive an undeserved thrashing. The classroom brawl on that occasion had been instigated by Magnus Reisen. But it was Chase who got the blame. The bullying Swede had paid the price for it after school, a discoloured nose ample proof to all of his devious chicanery.

Chase Farlow had arrived in Quemado two years before. Initially he had just been drifting through. But an

9

incident had occurred that quickly established him as a no-nonsense gunfighter when he thwarted a robbery of the assay office.

As a result, he had been offered the job of town marshal which had become vacant. The recent incumbent had been shot down by drunken roughnecks. Quemado had been taken over by lawless elements who mocked any attempt to curb their excesses.

Chase was no newcomer to the legal profession. He had worn the coveted tin star in numerous frontier towns with pride. Glowing testimonials as to his reputation helped secure the post. But the job of taming Quemado needed two men. Chase had accepted the job on that proviso. He had recently heard that his old partner, Buck Ramsey, was operating a gold claim in the mining camp of El Morro in the mountain country to the north. Chase headed up there without delay.

The two close friends had been through the war together. Fighting side by side in most of the major clashes, they judged themselves to be extremely fortunate to have survived the brutal struggle when peace was finally signed in 1865.

Following the cessation of hostilities, he and Buck had headed west in search of adventure. The terrible conflict had left them, and many others, unable to resettle into the humdrum world of dirt farming and domesticity. Numerous brushes with the law had followed until Chase had decided to follow a straight and narrow trail. Guilt was eating away at him like a cancerous growth. Stealing money from hard-working folk and living the high life at their expense did not sit well on his broad shoulders.

Buck, on the other hand, had no such compunctions. He was still eager to make his fortune, however that might be achieved. Inside or outside the law made no difference to him. So he headed for Colorado where a large gold strike had been made at Cripple Creek.

The parting of the ways for the two

close buddies had been somewhat fractious. Harsh words were exchanged. Since then, Buck had drifted across the Western territories, trying his luck in numerous boom camps without much success.

It had been three years since they last met up. Buck had since quit El Morro after having been suckered into buying a played-out claim. The chiselling swindler had met with an untimely accident in a ravine when Buck finally caught up with him. He was on his way south when the two old buddies unexpectedly ran across each other in the town of Bluewater.

The meeting had been emotional for both men. They had got hopelessly drunk and cried on each other's shoulder, much to the puzzlement of the Elkhorn Saloon's regular patrons. Such displays of feeling were usually kept firmly under control in the tough frontier settlements.

The saloon girls, however, welcomed the unexpected softening of the male libido and rewarded them both in the appropriate fashion later that night. Next day over breakfast, Buck revealed that he was down on his luck, having frittered away his latest acquisition of pay dirt. So he readily accepted his old buddy's offer of a deputy town marshal's job in Quemado, where Chase had recently been appointed.

The town was growing but had unfortunately attracted riff-raff from far and wide. All of the incomers were eager to strike it rich any way they could. Chase needed a man he could trust to help clear the place up and make it safe for law-abiding citizens.

It took three months of single-minded effort where a bullet in the back was ever present. But their dedication had finally paid off. The duo had effectively tamed the lawless elements that had threatened to over-whelm the mining town. Outlaws, carpetbaggers and other troublemakers had been sent packing. Thereafter, the town was able to settle down into a peaceful co-existence with the remaining miners.

That was when the rot set in for Buck Ramsey. The old army veteran needed the exciting buzz of placer mining to make life worth living. Not to mention the rewards accruing from a successful claim. Consequently, Buck had soon moved on. The lame excuse offered was that a lawman's pay was insufficient for the dangers involved.

So once again the two had parted company.

# 2

## INQUISITION

Awaiting his unwelcome inquisition, Chase pondered over how his buddy was faring. He had not heard from Buck in some time. The last wire said that Buck had once again struck it rich up near Gunnison in Colorado. On this occasion it was Buck Ramsey who was urging his old partner to join him. For a few days, the marshal had been tempted to leave Quemado and head north.

Duty, however, had finally prevailed. Chase Farlow felt responsible for the town that had given him the prestigious job of town marshal, thus enabling him to re-establish his self-respect.

Reluctantly, his mind returned to the current depressing situation into which he had fallen. Much as he tried to justify his actions, it did not bode well. Suddenly, a voice cut into his ruminations, curtly summoning him to enter the lion's den.

'The council are ready for you now, Marshal Farlow.' It was Aiden Crawley who ran the saddle and harness store. They were supposed to be friends. But the formal behest to enter the chamber was laced with icy disdain. 'Follow me.'

This was the first time Chase had seen the guy in his Sunday best suit. He looked like a tailor's dummy. He couldn't resist a wry smirk along with a suitably witty retort.

'Just stepped out of Jordan's window, Aiden?' Even as he uttered the biting gibe, the marshal regretted it. This was not the time for smart remarks, and certainly not the way to butter up a member of the town council.

Crawley merely flicked his large head towards the door. Even before he entered the council chamber, Chase knew which way the wind was blowing.

The writing was well and truly on the wall.

Abner Stanton was seated at the head of the long table, his back straight. A curling smirk warped his oily features. He was not about to let this opportunity pass. No offer to sit down was made. Chase just stood there twiddling his hat.

He knew that the sly official wanted him out. The mayor had been flattering and eager to please when his town had been overrun by troublemakers. But once the dust had settled, his attitude had changed. Chase cast a bleak look over the eleven faces staring back at him. Their grim expressions said it all. The culprit was left in no doubt that judgement had already been passed. The hearing that followed would be a charade. A bogus display of civic duty, ostensibly to give him a fair hearing.

'So, Marshal,' the mayor declared, squaring his shoulders while effecting his most sardonic of attitudes. 'You know why you are here. What excuse can you give for shooting down an innocent young boy?'

Chase felt like blurting out that the kid was no virtuous greenhorn. He was a thief who had been caught in the act. Sure, the shooting was a mistake. But it had been necessary given the circumstances. The words were on his tongue. Thankfully he managed to curtail the virulent outburst.

Nevertheless, Chase still attempted a spirited declaration to clear his good name.

He laid stress on the ostler's assertion that a robbery had been taking place. And with the gun store being the target, stern and decisive action was merited. Two warnings for the thieves to surrender had been given and ignored. What choice was he left with but to open fire?

The entreaty had no effect. It was like talking to a brick wall. The die was well and truly cast. And it was Snake Eyes that had turned up. No amount of reasoning was going to persuade Mayor

Stanton that his marshal's action had been justified.

Only one voice was raised in support of the marshal. But even a local notary like Doc Watson's plea for clemency had fallen on deaf ears. Chase's only real friend and ally on the council shrugged his shoulders. The gesture indicated that he had tried his best, but to no avail.

Stanton was well aware that his son was a young tearaway, and heading for a fall. Only the previous day the kid had been sent home from school for fighting. But the mayor was not about to let this opportunity slip through his greasy fingers.

For months he had been angling for a reason to get rid of the lawman. Chase had asked for a rise in the percentage rake-off from rents. The request had been refused.

His deputy was Mayor Stanton's nephew. The younger man was Stanton's choice. The veteran lawman would never have appointed a known hothead like Tate Hogan. He was too handy by far with those twin Colt Frontiers slung around his trim waist.

'When you gonna lever that old jackass out of his chair, Abner?' the deputy had complained yet again only the previous day. To Hogan, anybody over the age of fifty was a has-been and should be put out to grass. 'A guy that resorts to eye glasses ain't fit to wear a tin star.'

The marshal had once again been checking the accounts ledger when his deputy had lurched into the office, catching him wearing the spectacles. Chase was only one year past Hogan's cut-off point of fifty and had indeed started to feel his age.

His distance vision was perfect and he could still shoot straight. Nor had his draw been impeded by the passage of time. Having to wear spectacles for reading, however, was an affliction he had tried to keep under wraps, even though it had never affected his ability to keep order.

The deputy had been quick to inform his uncle of this startling revelation regarding the marshal's failing eyesight. It was sheer bad luck that Tate had caught him at a bad moment. He silently cursed the kid's sudden appearance before he could remove them.

On being informed, Stanton had aimed a bleak scowl at his sister's offspring. Nobody spoke to the town's leading official like that.

'Hold your tongue, boy!' he growled. But Tate was kin, so he kept his rising temper in check.

The news was indeed welcome and one more black mark against the aging lawman. But it was still an insufficient reason to remove him from office. The mayor was a canny fox. He recognized that a far more cogent excuse was required to convince the council that Tate should supersede the legendary gunfighter. Chase Farlow was well-respected.

His sister's constant bleating for Tate to get the full marshal's job was wearing him down. There was also Farlow's age to be considered and his request for a rise. Most significant of all though, as far as the mayor was concerned, were the significant gambling debts he had accrued with Brett Sinclair, who ran the Fairplay saloon.

Sinclair had promised to keep the debt secret providing it was repaid soon. But the marshal and he were close buddies. It was only a matter of time before the mayor's dubious handicap became public knowledge. Getting grid of Farlow would give him some breathing space.

Stanton angled a cynical grimace at the man now standing before him. A young boy who just happened to be his own son was now going to be the marshal's downfall. The mayor had unwittingly been presented with the golden opportunity for which he had been angling.

After the interrogation was over, Chase was told to wait outside while his fate was discussed by the council.

But the mayor was not about to let this opportunity slip through his fingers. Abner Stanton had the ability to talk his way out of a locked room. The gullible mooncalves on the council were child's play. He soon had them dancing to his tune. The icing on the cake had been to promise them a raise in expenses.

A vote was taken. The result would have been unanimous but for the dissention of Doc Watson. Stanton silently made a note to ensure the rebellious medic was voted off the council at the forthcoming elections.

When called back to hear the expected verdict, Chase stared at the wall, maintaining a blank expression as it was read out by the clerk of the council.

'Charles Farlow, you have been found severely wanting in the execution of your duty as town marshal of Quemado,' the unctuous toady burbled. 'It is the unanimous decision . . . '

Doc Watson's back stiffened. His vote

had been overruled. But he remained silent. ' . . . of the council that you be removed from office forthwith.'

Chase Farlow was given no opportunity to comment. The clerk ordered him to immediately surrender his badge and vacate the premises supplied with the job. He would be paid until the end of the month, but no testimonial as to his previous unblemished conduct would be supplied.

There was nothing more to say. Chase left the council chamber in disgrace. Shooting down a kid is not something that anybody was prepared to forgive or forget. It had effectively undone all his previous exemplary work.

Gathering up his meagre possessions, Chase left Quemado within the hour. Hostile eyes followed the tarnished ex-lawman as he mounted up and turned his horse north. His record of unsullied service in the name of law and order was forgotten. Mayor Stanton had effectively seen to that.

No doubt the skulking rat would be wiring other towns to ensure the bleak incident was spread far and wide.

At least Chase managed to keep his head held high as he nudged the chestnut down the middle of the street. Eyes firmly glued to the distant horizon of the Datil Mountains, he spurred off into the late afternoon sun.

# 3

## NO ROOM AT THE INN

Few travellers were encountered after he left Quemado, which was how Chase preferred it. He had no wish to explain his sudden departure, needing the solitude to contemplate an ambiguous future.

On the third day out, an entertaining night's supper was spent with a pair of garrulous trappers heading up into the San Juan Mountains. Their tales of derring-do involving grizzly bears and rabid wolves allowed Chase to forget his recent troubles for a brief spell. They parted the next morning as the early sun breasted the broken desert terrain of soaring sandstone buttes and flat-topped mesas.

Late that day, Chase spotted a line of Navahos silhouetted against the azure firmament. He gave them a wide berth. No sense asking for trouble even though the tribes were relatively settled at that time. This group appeared to be moving camp judging by the heavily laden travoises, led by squaws toting papooses on their backs. A young boy was herding a flock of sheep at the rear.

Chase pondered how these native redskins managed to wrest a living from the bleak wilderness. Water was like gold in this arid terrain. Springs and wells received names attesting to their vital importance to the desert inhabitants.

Five days later, the ex-marshal and now drifter finally reached the most northerly river in New Mexico. The San Juan was crossed by means of a ferry close to the town of Bloomfield. After leaving the ruins of an ancient Aztec Indian settlement, he followed the left bank of the Animas Tributary. Where the trail crossed the river, a faded sign was all that indicated this was the 37th parallel and he had entered the territory of Colorado.

A steady ride across the rolling sagebrush plateau brought the wandering rider to the first major town he encountered since leaving Quemado.

Durango was a typical settlement catering to the needs of both miners and cattle ranchers. Chase was confident that he would be able to secure a deputy's job in such a well-established township. The place certainly appeared to be booming. Wagons piled high with pit props and tools trundled along the main street. Shambling prospectors leading heavily laden burros added to the chaotic mêlée.

Behind the town's large ore smelter, high mountains reared up, their steep slopes draped in ponderosa pine. Thick smoke from the mill rose into the air, creating an artificial belt of cloud that hung like a death pall over everything.

Chase eased his way along the crowded thoroughfare, eyes peeled for the all-important sign advertising the lawman's domain. He had barely penetrated the dense throng when a raucous yipping cut through the general hubbub issuing from myriad throats. Pedestrians and horsemen alike scurried for the safety of the boardwalks. Seconds later, Chase was upended off his horse as two galloping riders bundled him out of their way.

An old prospector helped him up.

'It's two of that damn blasted Maggrie crew again.' T-Bone Craddock shook a fist at the disappearing duo as they continued to career along the street at breakneck speed scattering everybody in their wake. 'Every darned time they come down from Hesperus, the varmints use Durango's main street as a race track.'

Chase dusted himself down. 'Why doesn't the local sheriff do anything about it?' he asked.

'Buggy Johnson claims that he has too much on his plate. He can't be bothered with a couple of tear-aways,' Craddock scoffed. 'Like as not, he'll be propping up the bar at the Whale Tail Saloon chatting to the latest calico queen.'

'What about his deputy?'

'He ain't got one.' T-Bone shrugged. 'Don't know why. The council certainly has enough dough coming in to pay another wage.'

Chase cocked an ear at this piece of news. Perhaps this was to be his lucky day after all. And one way to impress Sheriff Johnson was to help him out. He hitched up his gun belt and stepped out into the empty street.

'I wouldn't do that, mister,' T-Bone warned. 'Them Maggries will be heading back this way in a minute.'

'Then I'd better be ready to meet them.' A fixed look of determination had settled over the tall man's craggy façade. He removed the Winchester carbine from its saddle boot and jacked in a round. The long gun was held loosely across his chest as he stood waiting in the middle of the street. He turned to face north.

'Sooner you than me, fella,' muttered the old guy, keeping well back.

A crowd of other bystanders paused in their stride as the lone gunman stood ready. Durango was not without its regular share of violent incidents. But this was a sight that the town had never previously witnessed. And it quickly drew more curious onlookers. Within moments, the sidewalks were lined with avid spectators, all eager to witness the outcome of this bizarre face-off.

Energized shouts of exhilaration could be heard at the far end of Main Street as the two competitors wheeled about, ready for their final dash. The loser had to fund drinks and dames that night.

As they came into view, it was clear even through the pall of dust that they were both neck and neck. The lone figure further down the street remained unmoving, a bluff and immoveable statue the pair had failed to notice.

When it seemed they would run him down, Chase Farlow swung the rifle to his right shoulder and levered off two rapid fire shots. The first removed the hat of one rider, the second a chunk from the other's left ear. Both men were taken completely by surprise.

Silas Maggrie screamed, clapping a hand to his damaged ear. Both horses faltered, instinctively veering to one side and colliding. Shocked and disorientated by this sudden interruption to their monthly contest, Fester let go of the reins. He fell to the ground, unbalanced.

Chase wasted no time in assessing the damage caused. He strode purposefully across to the muddle-headed pair, removing their hardware and tossing the pistols across to an equally stunned T-Bone Craddock. 'Look after their hoglegs, old-timer, while we escort these hellraisers to the jailhouse. Which way is it?'

'Follow me!' exclaimed the jubilant prospector. Suddenly all eyes were on the sourdough miner. He felt like a million dollars. Head held high, he strutted off along the middle of the street, leading the strange procession. Forcing the two crestfallen racers to their feet, Winchester in one hand and a Peacemaker in the other, Chase urged them onwards.

A round of thunderous applause erupted from the bystanders. This was a tale to relate over and over in the saloons of the town. The sorry duo was far too shocked by their sudden upheaval to complain as they stumbled along behind the miner.

Only when they were safely locked away in the town's hoosegow did they give voice to their resentment. A couple of shots into the ceiling of their cell by Sheriff Buggy Johnson soon curtailed the ranting.

'Much obliged for helping out, mister,' the lawman said. His congratulations were, however, rather muted. 'Those trappers needed bringing down a peg or two. Although I would have done it myself if'n I hadn't been busy elsewhere.' He didn't elucidate as to what that other engagement had been.

Chase held a cynical grin in check. T-Bone Craddock had specified exactly where he figured the star packer had been spending his working hours.

'An old prospector said they were from Hesperus,' Chase probed, accepting a cigar from the marshal.

Johnson nodded as he lit up. 'There are four brothers, plus a heap of other scumbags living in a camp up in the Sierras. They trap beaver and anything else they can catch.' The lawman paused, a jaundiced look of distaste souring his face. 'Had me a notion to visit the place some time back when Wolf Maggrie went crazy in the Speckled Hen House on the edge of town. Cut up one of the girls real bad.' He shook his head. 'Never again. That place is a law unto itself.'

'Maybe you need a deputy to help out,' Chase gingerly suggested.

'Could be you're right,' Johnson concurred. 'This town is growing fast.' A raised eyebrow silently appraised the speaker. 'You ain't touting for the job by any chance are you, Mister . . . erm, didn't catch your handle?'

'The name is Chase Farlow. And yep, I have some experience of the work.' Although he had no intention of explaining the reason for vacating his previous position. He slung a thumb towards the cellblock. 'You've already seen that I'm well capable of handling difficult situations . . . '

He never managed to get any further with his self-proclaiming testimonial. The marshal was on his feet.

'Sorry, fella, but I ain't hiring at the moment.' He proceeded to shuffle some papers about on his desk. 'I'm obliged for your help, but I'm a busy man.' The interview was clearly over before it had even begun. What had suddenly turned the atmosphere so decidedly frosty?

Then it struck the visitor like a hard gun barrel to the back of the head. The sheriff must have received a wire from Stanton. The scheming bastard had clearly sent them to all the towns within a week's ride warning of Chase Farlow's felony. And doubtless he had laid it on thick, judging by Buggy Johnson's reaction when he had given his name.

'So Abner Stanton has been hard at work blackening my name?' he rasped out.

'Don't know what you mean,' the lawman denied but he could not hold the other's withering glare.

'Whatever he's said is all a big mistake,' Chase countered.

'Are you refuting that it was your gun that resulted in a kid being gunned down?' Johnson snapped back. His previous denial was forgotten.

Chase had no answer. Sure he could have explained the circumstances. But this guy would not have believed him. It was pointless continuing. He stood up and headed for the door. That only served to stiffen Johnson's backbone.

'We don't want any lowlife child killer in Durango,' he snarled accusingly. 'I want you out of town within the hour.'

Chase was about to remonstrate that the injury had been superficial but the lawman's blank features indicated that he would only be pissing into the wind. There was no arguing with a cable sent by a New Mexico town mayor.

He left the office in something of a daze. How many other towns had the cable been sent to? Was Chase Farlow to be labelled a pariah? All he could do was continue heading north and trust that he could outride the unwarranted disgrace.

Mounting up, he took a back trail out of Durango so as to avoid any need to explain himself to those who had witnessed the recent citizen's arrest. A half hour outside Durango and Chase's customary alertness had completely deserted him. The most inept of road agents could have gotten the drop on him, such was his lack of awareness. All he could assimilate was the pall of shame that now hung over him. His reputation was in tatters thanks to that single error of judgement.

It was only the constant snickering of his horse that alerted the rider to the fact that he was not alone. The chestnut had smelt the approach of another horse. It was the rider's sudden appearance by his side that saw Chase grabbing for his gun.

# 4

## NIGHT OWLS!

'Easy there, mister,' burbled T-Bone Craddock, raising his hand to show his intentions were honourable. 'We're both heading the same way. Thought perhaps we could ride together for a spell — that is if'n you've a mind?'

Chase shrugged. Why not? Maybe unburdening himself to the old dude would help relieve the abject depression into which he had sunk. They camped out on the banks of the Animas with the San Juan Mountains soaring up on either side of the deep cut valley. Vast stands of aspen marched down the precipitous slopes hugging the shoreline. A fire was lit and strips of bacon cooked on a griddle. Coffee was soon on the boil. Normally it would have been an idyllic way to spend time with an associate.

But Chase Farlow was anything but contented. As he chewed on the crispy strips and shovelled down the pinto beans, his mood became ever more despondent. But at least after smoking a stogie and talking himself out, he felt better for the telling. Craddock listened without interruption. Once the whole sorry episode had been aired, the prospector considered the implications of the confession before responding.

Apart from an owl's soothing hoot from a nearby tree, all was peaceful and quiet.

'I can see how it might look to an outsider,' he declared thoughtfully. 'But now I know the full story, my view is that you ain't got nothing to reproach yourself for. It was an accident, pure and simple. Nobody can deny that a robbery was taking place. And your job was to apprehend the culprits. It's just bad luck that a kid was involved who happened to be the mayor's son. The guy wanted you out the way. In my view, those jumped-up turkeys have far too much power.'

Craddock paused to light up a briar. He stoked the strong concoction, watching the younger man's reaction to his verdict. Making to consolidate on his wise decree, the prospector added, 'Nobody was killed, nor even badly injured. You can hold your head high knowing that duty was fulfilled. And don't let anybody thumb their noses at you. Buggy Johnson is a lazy critter. Any deputy of that idler would have ended up doing all the work while he took the acclaim. You're well out of it.'

The old guy's vehement support lifted Chase's spirits.

'I sure am grateful for your counsel, old-timer,' he averred, genuinely moved by T-Bone's measured and sincere opinion.

'Old age don't always have to mean just grey hair and creaking bones,' the astute miner retorted. 'We elders have a lifetime's experience of making our own mistakes to call on. The trick is to make sure you learn from them.'

Chase went to sleep in a far more settled frame of mind. It was in the early hours that he arose and stuck a couple more branches on to the dying fire. Then he sauntered into a thicket to relieve a straining bladder. Too much coffee laced with whiskey. But a satisfying awareness of well-being had eased away the depression of recent times. And it was all down to T-Bone Craddock.

Chase rolled a stogie and stuck it in his mouth. The moon had reached its zenith in the night sky, an ethereal glow spreading sinuous fingers across the valley. Framed between the twin peaks of Engineer Mountain, the silver disc presented a hauntingly beautiful tableau. One that Chase could truly appreciate. The moonlight brought the landscape into sharp relief. Trees and rocky buttresses were etched in black. Lone effigies, silent and unmoving.

His hand paused, the unlit stogie drooping from his mouth. A man could get used to this country. The muscular frame rippled with a gentle sigh of contentment. Life could indeed be good once again.

But all was not as it seemed. Within the perfect Nirvana, a venomous serpent was stirring. The watcher's clear distance vision had picked out movement over on the far side of the camp. Instantly, the languid air of indulgence was discarded.

They were not alone. And with no call given to warn the campers of approaching visitors, only one conclusion could be drawn.

An ambush!

As if on cue, orange tongues of flame sliced apart the umber cloak of darkness. The silence was torn asunder, hot lead seeking out the oblivious sleeping forms. Bullets thudded into the nearest bed roll. Grunts of satisfaction issued from rasping throats. Pure luck had seen fit to remove the intended victim from a sure fire and violent demise. It was a lucky streak that Chase had seen fit to stay his hand when about to light up the stogie, which was now tossed aside.

Momentarily stunned by the sudden attack, Chase's natural instinct soon kicked in. A reaching hand grasped the Winchester resting against a tree trunk. The comforting presence of the rifle was a normal precaution when straying outside the influence of a camp fire. Wandering predators were never far away. Usually that would have meant bears or mountain lions. Those of a human variety were a shock to the system.

Who could be wanting to rob a pair of down-at-heel drifters?

This was not the time for cogitating on that premise. The gun rose. Lever, aim and fire! Lever, aim and fire! Half the load was despatched towards the clear targets in a matter of seconds.

Chase had the satisfaction of hearing a sharp cry of pain. One of the skunks at least had been hit. The advancing silhouettes were halted in their tracks.

Panic-stricken muttering saw them scuttling backwards into the shelter of the trees on the far side of the clearing. What had no doubt seemed an easy heist had suddenly been overturned.

A couple of slugs came his way. But they were off target. The skulking rats knew they had been rumbled and had no intention of making a fight of it.

More bullets pumped into the night as the barrel of the Winchester grew hot to the touch. Their intention was merely to deter the varmints from returning to finish their nefarious business. Chase hurried towards where he figured they had tied up. But he was too late.

Pounding hoofs indicted that the bushwhackers had heeded the rifle's deadly urging and fled the scene of their heinous endeavour. The moon, so recently a mixed blessing to the attackers, now acted as their saviour. Disappearing behind a cloud, it enabled the gunmen to merge into the opacity of night.

A grunt over on the far side of the smouldering fire stayed Chase's instinctive desire to pursue the felons. His sidekick had been hit. On returning to the camp site, he saw that the old guy had turned on his side, straight into the fire. Flames were already eating at T-Bone's straggly grey hair.

Chase leapt across the open sward and dragged Craddock off the fire. The hungry tentacles were quickly doused. Moans of anguish bubbled from the dazed prospector who was unaware of the danger into which he had rolled. Fortunately, no damage had been caused.

'Don't worry, T-Bone,' his saviour babbled out. 'I'll have you fixed up in no time.'

'What happened?' burbled the injured man, wincing as his benefactor cleaned the wound scoring his temple.

'Seems like some dudes wanted our supper,' Chase replied, trying to inject some levity into the harrowing situation. 'Your cooking must be renowned in these parts.' Blood was still pouring freely from the open head wound. But at least it was only a glancing blow. 'That sure is one helluva tough nut on your shoulders. The bullet would have finished off any normal jasper.'

The ashen features creased in what passed for a brief smile.

All Chase could do for the present was staunch the bleeding and dress the wound. The only item available was a rather grubby bandanna. It was long enough to wrap around the old-timer's head and would have to suffice until more permanent attention could be found.

Once T-Bone had been settled with a mug of fresh coffee in his hand, he voiced his own judgement of their recent brush with the grim reaper.

'I figure it was those two Maggries,' the prospector snarled, sipping the hot liquid fired up by a snort of whiskey. 'They must have been released from jail. Buggy Johnson likely issued a fine, then sent the varmints packing. The trail to Hesperus through the Sierras branches off from Coal Bank Pass some ten miles north of here at the head of the valley. Our fire must have attracted them. So they figured on some easy pickings.' He paused for a breather. 'Lucky for us you were taking a leak at the time. Those yeller bellies must have received the shock of their miserable lives when Marshal Chase Farlow kicked 'em up the butt.'

'Maybe I should pay this dump a visit,' Chase murmured, half to himself. 'White trash like them need teaching a lesson in trail camp behaviour.'

The response was a vehement shake of the head. 'Buggy Johnson was right about that rat's nest being a dangerous place. My advice is to set this down to experience and move on. Those guys can play real dirty.'

Although he did not articulate his thoughts, Chase's gritty regard said it all. He could play the hard operator as well.

He was about to voice the notion to

his partner. But a low rumble indicated that Craddock had fallen asleep. Chase left him. The old-timer needed the rest. He moved across to where the horses were picketed and settled down, the carbine nestling across his chest. There would be no more sleep for him that night.

Next morning, Craddock felt much improved. His recovery was assisted by another liberal snort of whiskey in his coffee.

They struck camp when the sun was well over the rim of the Red Mountains. Back on the trail, Chase kept the pace down to a walk. Craddock's head felt like it was being squeezed tight. And that wound had started to leak blood again. After the first hour, the gradient started to rise as the trail twisted up through Hermosa Gorge. Surging towers of rock on either side hemmed in the trail, forcing the riders down to single file. It was with some relief that they arrived at the crest where Cold Bank Pass marked the down turn.

Silverton was another two days' ride north. That was the nearest place where a permanent doctor would be in residence. Around mid-afternoon, Chase noticed a small farm on the far side of the valley. He headed over, hoping to get help for T-Bone. A man came out to greet them. He ambled across raising an arm in welcome.

'Howdy there, strangers,' said the farmer. 'Care to step down and join me and my pa for some vittles? We're just about to have supper. It's simple but wholesome.'

Chase's eyes widened. The lilting cadence had thrown him. On closer inspection, the guy turned out to be a gal. Even an ageing dude like Chase Farlow could appreciate the curvature of the lady's contours beneath the grey flannel shirt and slouch hat.

The girl laughed as a red flush spread across the newcomer's face.

'Don't worry about it, mister,' she said, capably allaying his discomfiture. 'Happens every time a new visitor calls by and I'm still in my working duds. The name is Della Speinkampf. I live here with my father. He's out in the meadow gathering in a crop of squash. He'll be back soon. Pa never misses a meal.'

'The offer is mighty kind of you, ma'am,' Chase announced, drawing to a halt outside a well-constructed log cabin. A hay barn in good repair indicated that the farm was well-run. 'But my partner here is in need of some doctoring. He's been shot up by a pair of bushwhackers who tried to rob us back down the trail.'

The girl's mouth dropped open on hearing this startling news. She hurried over and helped T-Bone off his horse. The old guy almost fell into their arms. It was clear that he had lost a heap of blood. Chase lifted him up and followed the girl into the cabin.

'He can have my room,' she declared, ushering them both into the rear bed chamber. 'I have some experience of frontier medicine which includes bullet wounds and snake bites, as well as delivering babies. Before Ma died last year of the fever, I worked in the Silverton clinic for Doctor Raistrick.'

'That sure is our good fortune, ma'am.'

Without further ado, Della put some water on to boil and went in search of her medicine chest. The head wound was cleaned, dressed and a patent salve applied. An expertly tied bandage received murmurings of approval from the patient when viewed through a looking glass.

'Makes me look like one of them Indian princes I've seen pictures of,' he preened.

It was an hour later that Jacob Speinkampf returned from the fields. He was a bald-headed man of around Chase's age. His bluff features were the result of working outdoors in all weathers. A midwest accent had in it a hint of German. The Speinkampfs were immigrants who had come to the New World in the 1840s.

Chase immediately noticed that the man was clutching a heavily worn Bible. The Good Book went everywhere with the farmer.

'I see we have visitors, daughter,' he announced, having noticed the extra horses in the corral. 'Are they staying for supper?'

His tone of voice was less than cordial. Speinkampf was wary of any visitors and viewed them all with suspicion. Chase emerged from the bedroom, having checked on his partner. His sudden appearance startled the farmer.

'What are you doing in my daughter's room, mister?' The blunt question was more like an accusation. His derogatory glance shifted to the heavy gun on the man's hip.

'Mr Farlow's partner has been shot by bandits and I've let him have my room to rest up,' Della replied tartly. She was clearly expecting this less than cordial reaction from her belligerent father.

'Shot, you say?' The man's eyes glittered with hostility. 'Have you brought gunslingers into my house?' He didn't wait for a response. 'I want them out of here right now. This is a God-fearing home. Those who choose to live by the gun are not welcome here.'

'You can't refuse help to someone in difficulties, Pa,' Della retorted. 'That sure ain't in the Good Book you prize so highly.' Her snappy rejoinder was brittle and testy. She did not appear to share her father's high regard for the Word. 'Doesn't the good Lord urge his followers to help those in need? To lend a helping hand to the weary and distressed traveller?'

Speinkampf arrowed a sour look at his daughter. But he was reduced to a mumbled acceptance of her reproof. 'The injured man can stay until he is well enough to travel,' he grudgingly conceded, although managing to retain his self-respect by having the final word. Chase was left in no doubt that his continued presence was not wanted. 'You can share our table, stranger. But you must leave here after supper.'

Della tried remonstrating. A belt of sarcasm crept into her measured attempt at mediation. 'Why can't he sleep in the barn, Pa? That way his guns won't be anywhere near the house.'

But her father was adamant. His face was flushed and angry. 'Don't argue with me, daughter. Now go see to the supper. I'm hungry.'

Chase hastily butted in, having no wish to come between father and daughter, no matter how biased and intolerant the Bible-pusher's opinions were.

'I'm obliged for your hospitality, ma'am,' he said in a level tone. 'I have no wish to stay where I ain't welcome.'

After washing up outside at the horse trough, Chase unsaddled his horse and gave the animal a rub down. No objection had been raised from the farmer when he asked to grain and water the chestnut. Then he went back inside the cabin.

The simple meal was set down on a table. Only Speinkampf seemed unfazed by the frosty atmosphere.

Chase lifted a fork ready to get started, only to receive a further admonition from the bigoted farmer. 'There will be no eating at this table until we have given thanks for the food on offer.'

All three bowed their heads as the farmer dolefully said grace. The rest of the meal was conducted in silence.

Chase was glad to escape the stifling atmosphere of the biased household. Although not an ardent zealot himself, he harboured no ill-will against those who followed the religious trail. But surely the good Lord had not meant for his teachings to be so dogmatic and uncompromising.

Wasn't compassion and kindness to one's fellow man at the heart of the Good Book? This guy seemed to wallow in self-inflicted flagellation. It was as if life itself were a punishment to be endured until judgement day brought the final release.

From an early age, Chase had been taught the difference between right and wrong. And apart from a few slips along the way, he had always tried to live by that honourable code of behaviour. He felt sorry for the girl having to live in such a stifling atmosphere.

But when it came to the crunch, it was really none of his business.

After checking that T-Bone was comfortable, he wished the old guy well. Then he mounted up, ready to leave. He was about to swing away from the farmhouse when Della Speinkampf stopped him.

'Don't hold it against my father,' she said, appealing for the stranger's understanding. 'He means well. Following the literal word of the Bible controls his whole attitude to life. He doesn't mean to be so domineering. But violence of any kind brings out the demon inside his soul. He shies away from it, believing you should always bare the other cheek.'

'Seems to me, ma'am, that a bit of common sense and compromise wouldn't go amiss by those living in a wild and lonely place like this. You have to protect yourself. After all . . . ' A rueful smile moved the craggy jawline. ' . . . doesn't the good Lord help those who help themselves?'

With that poignant observation, he was thankful to be leaving the Speinkampf homestead. A wave of the hand and he nudged the chestnut across the open tract to rejoin the main trail.

The small town of Silverton was two days' ride to the north. Maybe there he would be safe from the vengeful searching of Abner Stanton.

# 5

## A LUCKY BREAK

Dropping down the meandering route, Chase rounded a promontory to see the town of Silverton occupying a flat sward at the head of the Animas Valley. On one side stood the soaring pinnacle of Anvil Mountain. Opposite on the far side lay the towering range of the Sierra Negras. Numerous narrow trails could be seen winding up through the dense cloak of aspens. Hidden away were numerous mines where metals such as silver, zinc and lead were hewed from the rock.

Most sought after of all, however, was the yellow pay dirt, the acquisition of which all prospectors hoped would make them rich. However, only the lucky few were fortunate enough to achieve their goal. Most endured the back-breaking labour for little more than a pittance. But that did not stop them continuing to strive for that all important lucky strike. Such was the allure of gold.

Chase allowed the chestnut to pick her own way down the stony trail.

The main street was much like many others he had passed through. Mounds of debris littered the valley bottomland adjoining the river, where early attempts to extract ore had stumbled to a halt when the seams petered out.

Silver was the first metal to be mined in the valley. Charles Baker had made the discovery back in 1860. The cry of 'No gold! But silver by the ton!' was how the burgeoning settlement acquired its name.

By 1874 when Chase Farlow arrived, its reputation was well established. Perhaps he could secure a job here. A quick look around informed him that no telegraph lines had thus far reached into this remote enclave. So perhaps he would be in luck.

The first saloon was the Snake Bite. He drew the horse up to a free hitching post, tied off and entered through the bat-wing doors. There were few customers at that time of day. Most were probably still out in the hills, seeking to filter enough pay dirt to fund their night's carousel.

He shuffled over to the well-polished mahogany bar, where a pomaded bartender was busy applying an equally lustrous sheen to the back mirror.

'Be with you in a minute,' came the cheery greeting as the man buffed the finishing touches to the glass. Satisfied with his efforts, he stepped down off the chair.

'You've missed a bit,' declared the newcomer, pointing to a clean patch on the far side. The man frowned, peering at the indicated spot. He moved across and vigorously applied the cloth. 'Over there too,' came another piece of less than helpful advice.

The barman looked around. A dozen

drinkers were all staring in his direction, inane grins splitting their craggy faces.

'Ain't seen a barkeep caught by that trick since Ike Stanfield tried it on over in Telluride last fall,' declared a grizzled old-timer, chuckling into his beer glass. 'Well done, young fella.' Even though Chase was no spring chicken, this guy was his elder by at least ten years. Hard rock placer mining had no age barriers.

Greasy Grass Addison accepted the good-hearted bantering with nonchalant aplomb. He pushed a comb through the shiny locks that had given him the nickname. 'Maybe the joke will be on you, stranger, when I charge double.'

'Then maybe I'll have to find me another drinking den,' replied Chase, casually levering himself off the bar.

The beer puller raised his palms in genial surrender. 'OK, you win. Quits?'

Chase nodded. 'I'll have a large beer . . . at the normal price, of course.'

Once the drink had been poured,

Chase moved over to a table and sat down. Nursing the well-polished glass, he contemplated how best to approach the local star packer. Looking around the room, the recent banter had been forgotten as men continued with games of chance or reading the local news sheet.

Only one man was still studying the newcomer. He moved across and sat down opposite Chase.

'Have we met someplace before, stranger?' The man was well-dressed and sported a luxuriantly waxed ebony moustache. He was younger than Chase, but about the same height: six feet two and strongly built. He pushed his hat back, revealing startlingly deep brown eyes. Laughter lines on either side hinted at a lively sense of humour. 'I seem to recall your face from somewhere.'

A dark cloud settled over the newcomer's features. His bushy brows knitted together, probing eyes in shadow as they searched for answers.

Chase silently mouthed off a curse. Had that bastard Stanton gone and issued wanted posters with his picture on them? The skunk really was after his blood. So once again, it looked like he would be moving on sooner than expected.

'The name is Chase Farlow if'n you're interested,' he snapped out. 'Ex-town marshal of Quemado, New Mexico as I'm sure you are aware.'

The rasping retort went over the inquirer's head as he snapped his fingers. 'That's it. Now I remember. You were the hero that cleared the town of all its bad hats.'

The guy's face lit up. It was like he'd lost a dime and found a dollar. Somebody was actually pleased to meet Chase Farlow. There certainly did not appear to be any grudging animosity in the vibrant gesticulation. Perhaps his fall from grace had not reached this far north after all.

'The name is Will Bonney,' the man continued, displaying a broad smile. He held out a hand which Chase shook. It was firm and reassuring. 'I was passing through Quemado at the time heading up this way. That sure was one mean show you and that deputy put on. What brings you to Silverton?'

Now they were coming to the crux of the matter.

'I kinda fancied a change of scenery,' Chase declared, trying to present a blasé and detached mien. 'A guy can get set in his ways if'n he stays too long in one place, don't you think?'

'Couldn't agree more, Chase,' concurred Bonney. 'Although once you find a place that hits all the right notes, it's good to set down some roots. I reckon Silverton has all the qualifications I need, for the present at least. So were you hoping to find work here?'

Chase nodded. 'I was just about to visit the local tin star and see if'n he needed any help.'

Bonney shook his head. 'You're out of luck there. He already has a competent deputy in Clay Rambone.'

'Looks like I'll have to move on then,' Chase replied dolefully.

'Not necessarily.' The apologetic twist to Bonney's handsome visage was replaced by one of optimistic promise. 'I could sure use a guy of your experience.'

Chase gave the unexpected offer a wry twist of the lip. Deep-set eyes were trained on the man in uncompromising alertness.

'What kind of experience is it that you have in mind?' he asked bluntly, although he was pretty durned sure it was his gun hand.

'I'm in the ore assaying business. My main dealings are with miners bringing in the gold and silver they dig up. Naturally I need a man I can trust. Somebody who isn't going to have his head turned by handling large quantities of pay dirt. Gold especially is apt to turn a man's head. Even the most honest John can be mesmerized by the yellow peril.' The agent's penetrating gaze fastened on to his companion.

'Most folks around here say I'm a good judge of character. Far as I'm concerned, Chase Farlow is above reproach.'

The man in question almost felt Will Bonney was talking about a different person. If only he knew the truth, mused the ex-marshal. Would he still then have the same high opinion?

Bonney then went on to outline what had happened to bring about this situation.

'My regular man lit out only last week for some new diggings that have opened in the San Juans. Large nuggets of gold were discovered in Pole Creek and a new camp has grown up almost overnight. There's been a constant flow of eager prospectors heading that way, hoping to strike it lucky. They've called the place Eureka. The Sunnyside vein is reckoned to be the richest in this part of the territory. That's good news for us down here cos they ship the ore out through my company.'

'So what would be my job?' Chase inquired.

Bonney quickly filled him in. 'Once I've assessed the ore content brought in, the customer is then given a fair price. Your job is to keep records and bag it up, ready for shipment down to Durango. I'll pay you double what Sheriff Atkins would have managed, plus a percentage rake-off of all that we take in.'

Bonney eyed the other man closely, trying to assess his reaction. Having a guy with the credentials of Chase Farlow on the payroll would be a feather in his cap.

Chase stared ahead, giving nothing away. His features remained static, impassive. He slowly sipped his beer, pulling on a cigar as he mulled over the implications of staying on in Silverton. Perhaps it wasn't such a bad idea. At least it would allow the dust to settle, and his past indiscretions to fade. They say that time is a great healer.

Seeing that Farlow was wavering,

Bonney pressed home his advantage. His next comment was to further persuade the ex-marshal of his *bona fides*. 'Why not step over to the office? I can show you around. Then you'll be able to see how the operation works.'

Chase had already made up his mind. He turned and nodded. 'I'd be glad to work for you, Mr. Bonney. When do I start?'

Bonney clapped him on the back. 'Glad to have you on the team, Chase. You won't regret it.' Then evincing a hearty guffaw, he called for more drinks to clinch the deal. 'A bottle of French brandy over here, Greasy Grass. We got some celebrating to do. And now that we're going to be working together, call me Will.'

The two men later went across to the assay office where Chase's new employer proceeded to instruct him in the workings of Bonney Enterprises.

After the solid ore deposits had been ground down to dust, his first job was to collate, log and bag them up ready for transit. New samples were continually being brought in for assessment by miners, eager to hit that all-important big strike. Most were lucky to have riffled out enough specks of dust to keep them going. Major discoveries were certainly to be had. And it was the lure and excitement of making them that kept the miners hard at work.

The ore was kept in an iron safe. But holding large amounts of pay dirt on the premises was not conducive to an easy mind. Too much of a temptation for the denizens that always congregated in boom towns like Silverton. That was why a weekly trek down the Animas Valley was needed.

The following three weeks passed quickly.

The job was progressing satisfactorily and all seemed well with the world. Respect for his employer had risen sharply in Chase Farlow's estimation when Bonney had not batted an eye on discovering he wore spectacles for close work. That was in stark contrast to his dealings with Abner Stanton and his toad of a nephew.

He had also introduced himself to the local star packer. Joe Atkins accepted his story about seeking pastures new without comment. Nobody else in this remote enclave was likely to know anything about his fall from grace. Nor would they have cared anyhow. As with all mining settlements, gold and silver were all that mattered in Silverton.

Then suddenly everything changed overnight.

# 6

## BAD NEWS

Chase was propping up the bar in the Snake Bite when Bonney hustled through the bat-wings one evening. The grim look pasted across his face did not auger well. Chase feared the worst. He immediately jumped to the obvious conclusion. Bonney had somehow learnt of the shooting in Quemado. Maybe a passing drifter had let it slip. Chase nodded an acknowledgement but remained tight-lipped. He was resigned to packing up and having to move on.

However, the boss's dour regard was on account of something else entirely.

Bonney was in a quandary. It showed in his nervous delivery. Without preamble he reached across the bar for a bottle of whiskey, tipping a liberal slug down his throat. Needing a private word with his employee, he pulled Chase over to a side table beyond any listening ears. Miners were naturally inquisitive. Then he launched into what was bugging him.

'As you know, when these guys exchange their gold dust for hard cash, I have to transport the pay dirt down to the smelter.' He paused, swallowing nervously before continuing. 'But on the last couple of trips my drivers have been robbed. I didn't let on before cos I thought it was just a one-off heist. According to Joe Atkins, it's outside his jurisdiction. Only the county sheriff in Durango has the authority to go after these brigands. And that could take weeks.'

Chase sympathized. Buggy Johnson was not the most assiduous of lawmen when it came to law-breaking beyond the town limits as he had discovered. Bonney went on to declare that the robberies were bleeding him dry.

'None of my regular hauliers are

prepared to make the hazardous trek over Coal Bank Pass down to the smelter. They've been scared off.' The assay agent slung down another dose of mother's ruin. 'The ore is stacking up in the safe. As a result, funds are running low. If this continues, I'll be out of business in no time. I know it ain't your concern, but I desperately need somebody to accompany the next shipment.'

Bonney rubbed his hands. It was clear from the dark rings around his eyes that the problem had been giving him sleepless nights.

'You are the only guy available.' He was almost pleading for the ex-lawman's help and co-operation. 'Your skill with a gun is legendary and I know you won't be scared of mixing it with these brigands.'

The assay agent fixed an expectant eye on to the ex-marshal.

A wavering hesitancy showed on Chase's pinched features. Riding shotgun was a sight different to tally work.

He was an ex-lawman, not a mining guard. And the guy was right. It wasn't his concern.

He lit up the cigar offered by the assay agent. The reflective deliberation helped focus his thoughts. And it produced a shameful feeling of guilt. This guy had given him a well-paid job on the back of his past reputation. A high standing in place of his own bungled ineptitude. Few would have been prepared to do that. Chase Farlow owed him big time.

Bonney appeared to read his mind. 'And there'll be an extra percentage bonus when the goods are safely delivered. I figure the next haul should be done over the Sierra Negras to Ridgeway. The trek is longer but ought to be safer. The bandits won't be expecting a change of routine.'

Chase nodded although he was less optimistic regarding Bonney's confident assertion that the Sierras offered a heist-free route. These things had a nasty habit of getting out. Nevertheless, his mind was already made up.

'Reckon you've gotten yourself a deal, Will,' he said, accepting a glass of whiskey.

Of course, he would need help. One man toting a heap of metal ore had no chance of holding off a determined gang. It mattered little that he had once been a successful town-tamer. He was still only one man.

Buck Ramsey immediately came to mind. Some means would need to be found of contacting his old partner. The last he had heard, Buck was up north in Gunnison. Would he still be there? Where his old sidekick was concerned, you never could tell. And with Silverton not yet on the telegraph, how was he going to find out?

The dark frown tainting Chase's rugged contours was not lost on his new boss.

'Something on your mind, Chase?' Bonney asked as they sauntered across to the assay office. 'No point holding in any misgivings about the job. I know it will be tough. But you're the one guy I can depend on to see it through.'

'I'm gonna need another guy that I can trust to help me,' Chase declared somewhat sheepishly. 'Only trouble is being able to contact the right fella to cover my back.'

'I don't have any objections to another man accompanying you,' replied Bonney. 'It'll be just like a lawman taking on a deputy. So where is this guy?'

'Last I heard he was in Gunnison.'

'Well, it so happens that you're in luck.'

Bonney unlocked the door of the office and stepped inside, followed by Chase. He wandered over to the notice board and studied a particular sheet. A finger etched a path down the list of dates. Chase was intrigued.

'An express rider leaves here first thing tomorrow morning. He delivers the mail and any small valuables to camps on the far side of the mountains. And Gunnison is on his route. If'n your buddy is still there, we could have him back here by the end of the week.'

So that was how they managed to stay in touch with the outside world. It was slower than the telegraph, but would have to suffice until such time as the singing wires found their way over the Sierras. Talk in the town recently had been all about some surveyors who had been investigating just such a possibility. So it could only be a matter of time.

Chase had enjoyed the short time he had been in Silverton, but knew that it would soon be time to move on. Once this job was completed, perhaps he would join up with Buck in one of his mining ventures.

Chase Farlow was, therefore, more than eager to get started with his task.

Once the ore had been made ready for shipment with all the appropriate paperwork in order, Chase found himself at a loose end. It would be a few days before Buck arrived in Silverton, that was if'n he could be contacted. Otherwise, a replacement would have to be found. There were a heap too many of those ifs and buts to be considered. But there was nothing he could do about that now except wait.

This would be a good opportunity to visit the Speinkampf farm to see how T-Bone Craddock was faring. Bonney readily agreed to him taking a couple of days off.

On the way up to the lonely homestead, Chase pondered over the difficult task ahead. Thus far, luck had been on his side. He could only trust that his good fortune would continue. A prayer was offered up to the God that Jacob Speinkampf so much revered, although the farmer would have recoiled at the thought that his maker had been commandeered to watch over the transit of riches fought over by greedy humans.

When he reached the farm, Lady Luck, or maybe it was divine intervention, also appeared to be casting her spell over those he held in high regard.

Old T-Bone had fully recovered, thanks to the efficient doctoring of Della and her wholesome nutrition. By some strange quirk of fate, the old prospector was getting along well with her father. The two men happened to enjoy verbal sparring, which involved quotations from the Bible. Each tried to outdo the other in their mutual quest to come out on top.

Speinkampf had offered his new associate a job helping with the crops and tending the animals. It was work with which T-Bone was unfamiliar. But he welcomed the change of circumstances and readily set to, if at a somewhat sedate pace commensurate with his advancing years. The old-timer was busy converting the barn's loft into comfortable living quarters when Chase arrived.

The two greeted each other like long-lost buddies.

Chase was offered a bed for the night in the new bunk-up. Jacob Speinkampf had thankfully accepted that the tough lawman was in truth no threat to his bizarre interpretation of the Lord's Word. The two old travelling companions settled down in the warm hay.

The evening meal had been far more pleasurable than on his last visit. Perhaps T-Bone's presence was mellowing the strict zealot.

'Never figured you for a Bible-puncher, T-Bone,' Chase remarked as they burrowed into the soft hay quilt.

'My father was a travelling preacher back in Missouri,' replied Craddock. 'The Good Book was the only reading matter we had. So I got to know all the best bits. He was no fire and brimstone trail blazer. Pa enjoyed a drink the same as any other dude. But he brought us up to follow the Bible's teachings. That said, he always wore a loaded gun under his cassock. And he knew how to use it.'

Chase raised a quizzical eyebrow.

'Some bad guys once robbed the collection plate while he was in the church vestry.' The old boy laughed at the recollection. 'Pa chased them critters down Springfield's main street with nought but a Bible in his hand. He was hollering out for them to stop and threatening to summon the Good Lord's wrath down on their heads. Those guys were so scared, they dropped the dough and scarpered, expecting a bolt of lightning to strike them dead at any moment.'

The story elicited a bout of merry chuckling.

'What made you come west?' Chase inquired.

'Like all young fellers, I'd heard about the gold strike in California. Its lure was irresistible. Still is for that matter. Don't know how long I'll stick around here. But for the time being it's a good billet.'

And with that final comment, he turned over and was soon snoring happily. Chase went outside for a smoke before joining him. Rather than thinking back, his thoughts focused on the job he had taken on. It would be no simple delivery. Of that he was certain. A niggling at the back of his neck indicated that a difficult period lay ahead. It was a big responsibility he had accepted, perhaps more than he had bargained for. Will Bonney deserved his undivided support in ensuring its successful completion.

Next day, Chase left the farm, satisfied that all was as well as it could be with Della Speinkampf and his old associate. These two waved him off. But of the Bible-basher, there was no sign.

Circling behind the homestead to regain the main trail north, he saw the farmer kneeling before a shrine in a small fenced-off cemetery. Fresh flowers had been planted around the grave with a wooden cross at its head. The holy site was clearly a place of veneration for the distraught sodbuster. His head was bowed and he appeared to be reading a passage out loud to his deceased wife.

Her untimely death must have hit the

guy hard. Perhaps adhering to the literal translation of the Bible had helped him come to terms with the tragic loss. At that moment, Chase Farlow felt a sympathetic accord with the obsessive believer. He paused behind a tree, not wanting the guy to think he was being spied on.

After five minutes, Speinkampf got to his feet, touched the head of the cross and left the hallowed ground, his shoulders hunched and trembling. The hand clutching a white cloth was raised to his eyes. The poor critter was actually crying. Chase felt distinctly uncomfortable intruding on this overt display of personal grief.

His gaze followed the farmer as the man walked slowly back to the cabin. By the time he reached the door, his shoulders were squared, head held erect. The moment of abject heartache had passed, the mask replaced, until his next visit to the tiny memorial garden. Chase had unwittingly peered inside the very soul of a distraught human being and his own unique way of coping with tragedy.

With a heavy heart, and feeling a lot wiser, he turned away to continue his journey.

# 7

## OLD PALS' REUNION

Back in Silverton, the forlorn mood that had hung over him like a death shroud since leaving the Speinkampf holding was suddenly lifted. A most welcome sight greeted him outside the Snake Bite saloon. He moved over to the hitching rail and studied the Appaloosa with its distinctive white socks on three of the feet.

Ruffling the animal's ears, he said, 'Am I glad to see you, Dancer. Guess you being here must mean your boss is inside.' The horse snickered, its teeth baring in a welcome grin of accord. 'Recognize me then, do you?' Chase prattled, a beaming grin on his face. 'It's been some time since we last met up.'

His eyes shifted to the saloon. One

last pat for the horse and he stepped into the Snake Bite's gloomy interior. The broad back of his old buddy was instantly picked out among the line of drinkers at the bar. And he was still wearing that old sheepskin jacket. The lapel was raised as Buck Ramsey hunkered further into the warm coat. His broad shoulders shook, trying to disperse the chilly atmosphere.

It was still early May. And at this high altitude, the sun took its time rising above the enfolding circlet of mountains. A pot-bellied stove threw out heat from the middle of the room. But it only managed to reach those huddling close by.

Ramsey tossed down the whiskey chaser, gratefully imbibing its warming inner glow. The notion filtered through his brain that this might well be a deliberate ploy by the saloon owner to encourage his patrons to drink more.

The idle speculation was interrupted by a raucous belt of hallooing from behind.

'Old jaspers like you always feel the cold more.' The remark was followed by a ribald snort of jovial guffawing. 'Guess you must still be wearing those worn-out long johns as well as the sheep.'

Ramsey spun on the heels of his high-heeled riding boots. He would recognize that rowdy greeting anywhere. His leathery features remained inscrutable.

'Surprised you managed to find your way in here, speccy.'

Chase screwed up his eyes, pretending to feel his way over to the bar. The line of gaping men parted to give him room. He peered at the face coated with five days of grey stubble.

'Is that really you, me old buckaroo?' he croaked out in a deliberate antediluvian rattle.

For a full minute the two old friends held each other's gaze, neither moving a facial muscle. The rest of the Snake Bite's clientele were on edge. Everybody held their breath. Not a single cough, chuckle or grunt disturbed the heavy silence. How was this unexpected confrontation going to end? A shoot-out? Fists flying? Miners were always ready for bit of excitement to relieve the careworn existence of perpetual labour over a Long Tom.

It was Chase who brought the charade to its disquieting finale.

A muscle behind the left eye quivered. Then he burst out laughing. Ramsey joined in as the duo slapped each other on the back. He grabbed up the whiskey bottle and two glasses, ushering his old friend over to a table nearer the fire. Both men held out their hands to soak up the welcome heat.

Chase poured the drinks. 'Glad you could make it, Buck,' he intoned, genuinely pleased to have been reac-quainted with his old partner. 'Boy, it sure is good to see you after all this time. What have you been up to?'

The tension in the saloon drained away, along with any interest in the proceedings. Crabby mutterings soon dissolved as the other drinkers resumed their normal activities. There were to be no high jinks after all.

Ramsey opened his mouth to explain. 'Oh, this and that, you know.' He was about to expound but was not given the opportunity.

An aggrieved voice piped up behind the two amigos. 'Ain't you gonna introduce me, Buck? This jigger drags us away from a lucrative scheme we had going up in Gunnison. The least he can do is fill us in on this new deal.'

'And so he will, kid, so he will,' Ramsey mollified, smoothing out the feisty intruder's hackles. 'All in good time. Me and Chase go back aways. Too much time has passed since we last split the breeze. You sashay over yonder and keep that gal company while we talk things over. Practise them chat-up lines I gave you.' He pointed to a gaudily-clad escort talking to the piano player. 'I'll give you the nod when we're finished.'

The kid planted his feet squarely on

the floor and crossed his arms. He was not being shunted off that easily.

The sudden appearance of the young man had caught Chase on the hop. He hadn't reckoned on his old associate bringing company along. That wasn't meant to be part of the deal. So who was this kid? Was Buck figuring on including him in the action? These were questions that needed answering, and sooner rather than later.

'What's this all about?' he said as the kid pulled up a chair. 'I didn't know you had taken up with somebody else, Buck. Who is this guy?'

Ramsey then made the introductions. 'Chase Farlow, meet Gabe Strawtop.'

Chase's mouth dropped open. 'Gabe Strawtop?' he exclaimed, trying to restrain a biting guffaw. 'What kind of a handle is that?'

The kid bristled. His face turned bright red. A hand dropped to the gun on his hip.

'What's wrong with it, wrinkle-face?' he rasped, injecting his own blend of biting satire into the retaliation. 'At least I can walk down the street without the aid of a walking stick.'

Buck laughed out loud. 'The kid has a point. You sure ain't no spring chicken.'

Chase casually ran a languid eye over Ramsey's down-at-heel appearance.

'Guess neither one of us in the first flush of youth, that's true enough. I can see that you ain't visited a tailor recently.' He casually stuck a finger into a tear in the grubby fleece jacket, his nose flickering. 'It don't smell too sweet neither.' Then he leaned back in his chair, running a jaundiced eye over his buddy's cocky sidekick. 'Kind of a strange name, is all. Ain't come across no Strawtops before. Nor a Gabe neither.'

Ramsey filled him in. 'That's 'cos it ain't his real moniker. Take off your hat, boy.'

Strawtop frowned but did as bidden. His flowing locks were revealed in all their yellow glory. He was a good-looking kid, if a little prickly. 'And he sure has the gift of persuading folks to buy those pay dirt claims we've been peddling.' Buck's voice then dropped to a mysterious whisper. 'Only problem is, it don't stretch to chatting up the dames. One shows an interest and he clams up tighter than a banker's fist. I've been giving him some helpful tips.' Ramsey tapped his nose suggestively.

'You want help with the ladies, kid,' the ex-marshal advised mockingly, 'come to your Uncle Chase, not this old goat. All he can pull are ugly faces.'

The gentle ribbing was irking the young fellow. So Chase returned to his original query.

'But why choose a different name from that you were born with?'

'That's no business of your'n, mister,' rapped Strawtop, irritation still flaring at this badinage promoted at his expense. 'So keep your beaky conk out of the trough.'

'Now keep your hair on, Gabe. Chase don't mean nothing. He's just naturally got a big nose,' Ramsey placated, emitting a chuckle of his own. 'So why not just tell the man your real name.'

Now it was Strawtop's turn to play all coy. 'Do I have to, Buck?'

But Ramsey insisted, although he tempered the order with a modicum of sympathetic understanding. 'Reckon so, kid. It's bound to come out sometime.'

'The name is . . . Clarence M. Goodenough.'

'Clarence . . . M . . . Goodenough!' Chase burbled. He was dumbfounded. 'Where in the name of Old Nick do you come up with these monikers? So what does the M stand for?'

'Marion.' It was uttered in a sibilant croak as the kid looked around to ensure none of the other patrons had overheard.

'Marion???' Chase blurted out, now unable to contain his mirth. 'This only gets better and better.'

'Keep it down, can't you,' pleaded a panic-stricken Strawtop/Goodenough. 'Do you want the entire saloon to hear? I've had enough brawling to last me a lifetime. And I'm still only twenty-two.' His reaction suddenly changed to a biting caveat. 'But that don't mean I'll turn the other cheek like the Good Book suggests.'

Luckily, nobody appeared to have picked up that the word uttered was in reference to the kid's name. Nonetheless, Buck Ramsey felt it only right and fitting that he should come to his young partner's aid.

'His pa reckoned such a name would force the boy to defend himself against the school bully boys who would try to make fun of him. Reckoned it was the best way to toughen him up in the hard frontier world.'

'And it worked,' the kid interjected squaring his shoulders. 'Any dumbcluck who figures to make himself popular at my expense will get a pasting he won't forget.'

The blunt threat was clearly aimed at Chase Farlow. The older man held his hands up in surrender. He was impressed.

'Guess we'll stick to Gabe Strawtop then. Now that I've gotten used to it, it sure is a fine handle that any man would be proud of. Guess you're on the payroll along with grandpa here.'

Drinks were poured as the three partners settled down.

The two older men sitting opposite one another were like chalk and cheese. Chase pondered on how his old partner had teamed up with this testy young sprog. Buck appeared to have figured out his thinking.

'Guess you're wondering how we met up?' He then went on to elucidate. 'Gabe here was defending the family reputation against a group of drunken cowpokes in Gunnison's Powderhorn Saloon. There were four of them. He tried persuasion. But they were more than eager for a set-to. The kid felt that he couldn't disappoint them. And he was able to handle himself good, thanks to his pa's warped sense of how best to raise his kin. Two of the braggarts were nursing sore heads when one of the others figured to play dirty with a broken chair leg. That's when I decided to step in and make it a fair fight.'

Gabe Strawtop then butted in to finish the story. 'It was later over a drink that Buck here suggested it might be wise for me to adopt a more snappy handle. With my blond hair, Strawtop sounded good.'

'What made you team up?' Chase asked, enthralled by this unlikely pairing.

Strawtop again answered. 'After I deftly persuaded the saloon boss that those Crazy J cowpokes should foot the bill for the damage caused, Buck asked me to join him in selling digging claims for the West Elk Land Development Company.'

'I had the contacts, while Gabe here had the chat lines. And it was working a treat until we got your message.'

'So what happened to that big strike you told me about?' said Chase.

'Washed out like most of the others I've tried,' replied a glum Buck Ramsey.

'I found out the hard way that mining is for suckers. Selling claims is far more secure — '

'We just hope that you dragging us down here is gonna be worth the trip,' interrupted Strawtop, leaning across the table. His set regard was a potent challenge to the ageing ex-lawman to state his case.

'I'm sure that Chase here has good reason for seeking out an old partner. We always worked well together in the past, didn't we, buddy?'

Chase nodded. He had no argument with that.

'There's no reason why that can't continue,' Buck reasoned. 'So what's this all about?' Ramsey had quickly discarded the jovial repartee for a more serious mien. 'Your message gave nothing away. Just said you needed help and to come straight away. It sounded mighty intriguing. How about filling us in?'

'Be glad to, boys.'

Chase then went on to explain his

meeting with Will Bonney and the assay agent's need for escorts to accompany the forthcoming delivery over the Sierra Negras to Ridgeway. Buck Ramsey's face remained deadpan at the mention of the valuable cargo and the need for trustworthy guardians to escort the gold, following the recent spate of robberies. When Chase had finished, he sat back, allowing his associates to fully assimilate what was expected of them.

'So are you fellers in?' he asked eventually.

'Sounds like a tough proposition, buddy.' Ramsey was erring on the side of caution. 'Reckon I need to talk this over with my partner here before giving you our answer,' he muttered, nudging Strawtop to join him over at the bar.

Once they were nursing a fresh glass of beer, the kid deferred to his more experienced partner by posing the question now uppermost in his mind. 'Are you thinking about all that gold and what we could do with it, Buck? 'Cos the thought is sure nagging at me like an itchy flea bite.'

The notion had certainly not escaped the older man's attention. The brooding frown told Gabe Strawtop all he needed to know. He responded with a poignant nod. Then the older man issued a blunt warning. 'But I want Chase in on the heist. With your persuasive talents and my back-up, I reckon we can bring him round.'

'What if'n he won't play ball?' Strawtop augured pensively.

'Let's figure that out when and if the time comes.' Buck levered himself off the bar and pasted a half-genuine smile on his face. They sauntered back over to join their new employer. 'OK then, Chase, we're both in. When does the show get on the road?'

Will Bonney was initially somewhat reluctant to take on two extra men. Gabe Strawtop's silky tongue, however, soon persuaded him to approve Chase Farlow's choice of partners.

New guns were supplied by Bonney. The Colt Frontiers together with the latest .44.40 Winchesters brought howls of delight to the young guardian, who ceremoniously dumped his old Remington Rider pistol and Springfield breech loader into the Animas River.

They immediately headed down to the river to try out the new firearms. Testing them proved to be an exhilarating challenge as all three partners strove to outdo the others in their prowess.

Chase and Buck couldn't help but be enthused by their young buddy's fervid passion. They were both fascinated by Strawtop's dexterity with his new pistol. Tricky manoeuvres such as the Denver Shift and the Oklahoma Twist were performed with amazing panache. He finished by potting three tin cans sitting on a fence.

It was Chase who voiced the misgivings uppermost in both their minds. 'That's all very well, Gabe. But when the chips are down, will you be ready to shoot and maybe kill a human target?'

The boy's response was hesitant.

Clearly he had never shot a man before. Buck saw the wavering hint of uncertainty in his young partner's eyes and quickly came to his aid. 'He'll do the business if'n the need arises. You can be sure of that. Ain't it the case, Gabe?'

'Sure is,' averred the kid. Eager to prove his worth, Strawtop fanned the revolver at a passing buzzard. Deadly tongues of flame and lead spat skyward. The bird squawked once before plummeting to earth. A preening grimace of satisfaction split the youthful visage as he blew on the smoking barrel. 'Any jasper tries to take our gold, he can expect a similar hot reception.'

Chase quickly picked up on the kid's assumption and bluntly issued a mandate. 'Just remember that we're employed to tote the company's pay dirt. Don't get any bright ideas about it being up for grabs.'

Ramsey brushed off his old friend's warning as being a mere slip of the tongue. But a guarded look passed between the two deputy custodians.

The first shots had been fired and deftly deflected. Chase Farlow, it appeared, was going to be a tougher proposition to persuade than they had figured.

# 8

## UNEXPECTED ENCOUNTER

Over the next few days, preparations were put in play for the vital trek.

The morning of their departure was scheduled for sun up. Most of the town was still asleep. Will Bonney did not want to advertise this special delivery. That was probably how the bandits had gotten wind of the previous shipments. Especially now the goods were going to be packed over the Sierras to Ridgeway.

He explained in detail this lesser-known trail west through Pandora and Tomboy, avoiding the usual route by way of Coal Bank Pass. It was longer by a couple of days, but they were much less likely to encounter any trouble.

A pack mule was loaded with provisions for the week long trek. The ore was loaded on to a second mule at the final moment of departure. Horses and mules were tucked away out of sight in a stable behind the assay office. A variety of different metals were being carried including lead, zinc and copper. But the bulk was silver and gold.

It was the sight of the latter glittering in the early morning light that found young Gabe Strawtop salivating like a dog on heat. Ramsey was forced to issue a stark warning for his partner to keep his enthusiasm under wraps if their plan was not to crumble at the first hurdle.

'Keep them bulging peepers inside your head, boy,' he snapped, pulling Strawtop to one side where they were hidden by the horses. 'That ogling of your'n is gonna arouse suspicions as to our intentions before we even set out.'

'Sorry, Buck,' the kid apologized, casting a guilty glance towards their unwitting dupe. 'It's just seeing all that lovely pay dirt. I ain't never set eyes on that much in one place before. Makes a fella go all tingly inside.'

A sharp dig in the ribs brought the kid back to heel. Although Ramsey had been equally smitten by the eye-popping sight. He only hoped that his old buddy could be brought round to backing their play when the time came.

'You guys ready for mounting up yet?' an oblivious Chase Farlow called out from the far side of the corral. 'I'm all set over here.'

'We sure are, Chase,' Ramsey replied. 'Just checking on a loose cinch.' He pulled up the collar of the sheepskin against the raw chill of early morning. A final scowl of warning for Strawtop to hold his zeal in check, then he swung into the saddle. 'All set when you are, buddy.'

At that moment, Will Bonney emerged from the back door to offer a final piece of verbal encouragement to his men. 'You boys carry this through and there'll be a sizeable bonus in your pay packet. And like as not a permanent job if'n you want it.

Success is bound to attract other miners to ship their ore through my company. So good luck to you.'

The low jingle of saddle tack filtered through the blurry haze as the small party nudged their mounts out of the corral.

'This mist will help until you've left town,' was the final comment from Bonney as they silently moved off.

'We'll see you in about ten days, boss,' Chase assured the assay agent. 'I'll make sure the pay-out for the ore is lodged safely at the National Bank in Ridgeway.'

Within seconds, they were swallowed in the swirling tendrils of white drifting in the low breeze. At this time of year, it would be mid-morning before the mist finally cleared from the valley. For the first half hour, the gentle creak of saddle leather was all that disturbed the silence. Each man was cocooned in his own thoughts. Chase Farlow had not the slightest inkling that his ruminations diverged drastically from those of his two partners.

Soon the gradient began to steepen as they moved up through Sawpit Gorge. The trail was clear, but narrow. Progress was slow but steady as it twisted and turned between the tight stands of pine, lining the chattering creek to their left. Although Chase had not ventured this way before, Bonney had given him a comprehensive plan of the route. He was, therefore, able to lead the way with confidence.

Around mid-morning, they broke through the mist into bright sunshine. Its warming glow quickly suffused their chilled bodies, occasioning an altogether more mellow frame of mind. The starkly beautiful panoramic display of the Sierra Negras was a joy to behold. No man could be left unmoved by such a tableau of nature's hardware in all its scintillating glory.

They automatically drew to a halt on a ledge overlooking the deep chasm of Sawpit Gorge. Even a young tearaway like Gabe Strawtop was stunned.

'That sure is one mighty breath-taking view,' he mumbled in awe. The others could only nod their agreement.

'That must be Mount Wilson over yonder.' Chase studied his map then pointed to the jutting prow of the soaring mountain peak. 'We need to keep it on our left side all the time.'

'How's about a stop to brew up some coffee,' suggested Ramsey. 'My bones could sure use it. These mountain trails take it out of a fella. My butt ain't as tough as it once was.'

'Getting old, that's your trouble, Buck,' his young partner guffawed.

'Comes to us all, Gabe,' was the somewhat jaundiced reply. Then he brightened. 'Although I reckon even a whippersnapper like you wouldn't say no to a hot drink and some of Ma Bassett's stone cake biscuits.'

Over the snack, Buck Ramsey made his first gentle foray into teasing out his old partner's appetite for acquiring some easy dough.

'So things ain't been going too well

for you in recent times, eh, Chase?'

'You could say,' came back the stilted reply.

'Some guys in your position might figure the world owes them something for being treated so mean.' Ramsey eyed his buddy to gauge his reaction before adding, 'Slaving away for a pittance while scheming charlatans like that Stanton dude rake in all the profits. Don't seem fair to me.'

'A fella has to take what he figures is due to him. That's what I reckon is fair.' Strawtop's interjection was choked off on receiving a warning grimace from Ramsey to curb his tongue.

Chase thought for a moment before replying. 'So long as a man can hold his head up and buy his own beer with a clear conscience, that's all I'm asking for.'

It was not the response that his new associates would have wished. The guy was still that honest Joe of old. Honour and integrity meant everything to guys like Chase Farlow. It was going to be a struggle persuading him otherwise. But this was not the time to undermine that upright stance.

Chase harboured no reservations about his partners' wily connivance. He was a naturally trusting guy. And Ramsey respected him for that. Nonetheless, that wasn't going to stop him from working out some way of riding away with that gold before this trip was much older. Preferably with Chase participating on an equal basis. Otherwise . . .

He left that supposition open to further debate.

Two days later, the small party was well into the foothills leading up into the mountain fastness of the Sierra Negras. It was Strawtop's eagle-eye that spotted a lone rider on the trail up ahead. He immediately alerted his partners. The other traveller had joined their own trail from another forking in from the left. Like a piece of string, it could be seen winding up from Coal Bank Pass below through green fields speckled with clumps of golden columbine.

'Now where can that jasper be headed?' he muttered out loud. 'He ain't seen us. Do you fellas reckon we ought to give him a wide berth?'

They drew to a halt, watching the rider and studying the surrounding terrain to see if he had any company. Maybe he was one of the robbers who had spotted them and was figuring on how to grab their cargo.

Ten minutes later, Chase voiced their joint evaluation. 'Looks like he's alone. And headed in the direction of Hesperus. The guy ain't a threat to us.'

'Hesperus, you say?' exclaimed Ramsey. 'That's where those Maggrie brothers live, ain't it?'

Chase had filled his buddy in on T-Bone Craddock's suspicions after the attempted robbery beside the Animas. But that's all they were. Suspicions. No positive identification of the bushwhackers had been possible in the dark. So he made no comment, even though his mind was running along the same lines.

'Do we have to pass through that berg?' added Strawtop.

'It's the shortest route,' said Chase. 'But we could take the alternative trail over the Dallas Divide. It's longer by two days but would avoid the chance of any trouble.'

He spurred off. That decision would not have to be made until the following day. Had the tough ex-marshal not been responsible for their valuable consignment, he would have rode in there and challenged that Maggrie clan to prove their innocence.

But as things stood, he had not been given the choice. The safety of the shipment must take priority over any personal feud.

Another hour passed. All the while, they were steadily gaining height. The sun was rapidly losing its heat. Grey shadows marched across the landscape as day surrendered to dusk. As the trio drew closer to a section of level plateau land, the lone rider stopped to allow them to catch up.

Only when they were within hailing distance did Chase Farlow recognize the person concealed beneath the rough work clothes.

★　★　★

Della Speinkampf had been on tenterhooks all morning. She prayed that her father would head up to the north pasture to repair those fences about which he had been complaining. Trying to appear busy, mending holes in his spare jacket and fixing patches to the knees of frayed overalls was becoming increasingly irksome. Anxious eyes were forever straying to the track, slanting down the hillside from the direction of Hesperus.

It was a struggle to conceal her nervousness. Her palms were sweaty, skin prickly with suppressed tension. For Della was expecting the arrival of a visitor. And not just any old passer-by.

This guest was of the male variety!

For the last two months, she had been conducting a clandestine liaison with Danny Maggrie, the youngest of the notorious clan. They had been meeting at the Hermosa trading post which was a two hour wagon ride to the south-west.

At their last assignation, Danny had said he had something special to give her. It had been agreed between them that he should come to the farm on his way down the mountain trail from Hesperus. But only when her father was absent. Had Jacob gained even the faintest inkling that his daughter was involved, and with a Maggrie to boot, all hell would have broken loose.

In truth, nobody was good enough for his daughter. Only someone of the same temperament and inclinations as himself would stand a slim hope of winning her hand. Men considered good prospects in the marriage stakes were distinctly rare in the remote frontier settlements of Colorado. A couple approved by her father had been introduced in the last year. Both were stuffed shirts with little to commend them other than a penchant for quoting from the Bible.

That in itself was enough to scotch their prospects in Della's eyes. She craved excitement, love, affection. After secretly reading the romantic dime novels specifically aimed at the female audience, she yearned to be swept off her feet by some dashing hero. A flight of fancy to be sure, but Della was a dreamer.

When Danny Maggrie accidently chanced into her life during one of the supply trips to the trading post, she accorded him an iconic status far beyond his capacity to reciprocate. Without a doubt he was good-looking, and sported a certain earthy charm. But a harsh upbringing in the tough trappers' camp of Hesperus placed him well outside the august category that would have been approved by her father. The boy was rough around the edges, evincing a distinctly crude sense of humour.

On the first occasion they had met, Jacob had decided to remain at the farm where vital chores had to take priority. So this was one of the few times that Della made the trip on her own.

Chance had unwittingly brought them together at Hermosa. Coy looks and the odd word had led to a shared table in the trading post for the midday meal supplied by the proprietor's Ute Indian wife. Being the only visitors at that time meant that communication of some sort was inevitable. Talk had been stilted and desultory on that first meeting. But gradually the ice had thawed on subsequent encounters.

Danny had regaled her with daring tales of his hunting conquests. To any ordinary listener, these were clearly flights of fancy meant to impress. But Della was enthralled. The young trap-per was attentive and treated her as a woman, dispersing the dowdy image instilled by her father. He was certainly no ladies' man. And it was evident that Danny Maggrie was a tenderfoot in the gentle art of courtship. But Della was prepared to overlook such minor issues.

His principal redeeming feature was that he recognized her need for warmth and tenderness. Danny had paid Della more attention as a woman than she had ever received previously. She became putty in his calloused hands. Not that he tried to take advantage of her naïvety. He was equally inexperienced in that respect.

What trysts they managed during those early days were fleeting. Della invariably had her father to contend with. Consequently, only brief liaisons were possible over the coming weeks and months. But the connection had been made. And Della Speinkampf had woven a quixotic spell around the relationship, imbuing it with a hearts and flowers idealism.

The reality of having to live in a primitive camp populated by coarse and uncouth trappers was lost to her. All she wanted was to escape the suffocating oppression of her father's restraining influence. Danny Maggrie had provided the means of attaining her aspiration. And on their last meeting he had plighted his troth.

Today was his first visit to the farm. Della sighed. She could barely contain her impatience as her father fussed around. Silently she pleaded for him to depart to the north pasture. He would be there for most of the day.

T-Bone Craddock, who was now an integral part of their life, had early on begun to suspect that Della was involved in some clandestine plot. The girl's dreamy looks and heart-felt sighs, lost on her father, were quickly picked up by the wily old prospector. He suspected that a romantic assignation was at the nub of her feminine behaviour.

Unlike his boss, T-Bone sympathized. His thoughts harked back to similar situations over the years. Had he known the identity of the man in question, his offer to assist the girl would have followed a far more disparaging course.

It was T-Bone who persuaded Speinkampf of the need to be elsewhere at the time of the proposed rendezvous. When the long-expected day arrived, Della forced herself to remain calm. At long last Jacob Speinkampf made a move. Della heaved a sigh of relief. A brief look of accord passed between the girl and her co-conspirator.

As soon as Jacob had left the farm, she hurried outside and tied a red towel to the gatepost. A signal to Danny Maggrie that the coast was clear.

T-Bone also made himself scarce. This was no time for an old guy to be butting in on a romantic assignation.

# 9

## BEAR CLAW PROPOSAL

Darkness had fallen.

A silvery moon shone down from a clear sky, bathing the landscape in a ghostly yet mesmerising appeal. The camp had been established on a level sward sheltered from the cutting mountain wind by stands of aspen. Nevertheless it was still cold. The four people, three men together with the unexpected presence of Della Spein-kampf, huddled into their blankets.

It was not until they had finished eating that questions as to the girl's lone presence on this trail were asked. These initial forays into the girl's unexpected appearance were met with a firm rebuttal. Eventually, however, the whole story had tumbled out in a single gushing torrent of words. And the revelations were startling.

Only now did she pause.

Sipping the hot coffee, she sized up these three men, trying to judge their reactions as they mulled over what she had divulged. Chase Farlow was already known to her. And he had vouched for his buddy's veracity. So Della harboured no fears for her safety. Both men appeared circumspect. They had a job to do and were clearly wondering how her presence would complicate matters.

The young guy was different. Gabe Strawtop was particularly captivated by their guest. Although the girl's face was streaked with trail dirt, and her thick dark hair hung limp and straggly beneath the old felt hat, the kid knew that beneath the unkempt appearance was an attractive and desirable woman. The pair might be strangers, but after hearing her story, he still felt a stab of envy that another man had captured her heart.

It was Chase who voiced the question

uppermost in all their minds.

'So why are you heading up into the Sierras, Della?' he inquired gingerly. 'This is no place for a woman on her ownsome.'

Della shivered. And it was not on account of the chill in the air. Gabe misinterpreted the action. Hastening to play the concerned host, he removed his own coat and placed it gently around her shoulders. A grateful smile lit up her face, turning the boy's legs to jelly. He sat down quickly, struggling to hide his reddening features behind a raised hand.

She then continued with the rest of her sorry tale.

'For some reason, Pa came back early,' she iterated. Tears ran down her grimy cheeks as the whole sorry episode was resurrected. 'Danny had left by then, but I still had on my best Sunday dress. I didn't want to take it off. I was parading in front of the mirror and dancing around when he suddenly came in through the door. He was immediately suspicious, demanding to know why I was dressed up. Seeing the lipstick and rouge on my face sent him into a fit of rage.' A wail of agony bubbled up from her throat. 'I've never seen him like that before. It was terrifying. He was like a devil bewitched.'

She burst into tears, revealing the side of her face concealed by the hair. A purple bruise, livid and yellowing round the edges elicited sharp intakes of breath from the listeners.

'Your own father did that?' snarled Strawtop, jumping to his feet. 'I'll kill the rat.'

'Sit back down, boy!' Ramsey snapped. 'And control yourself. Go on, miss, you were saying.'

'That is the first time he has ever hit me,' she sobbed. Then a hard glint appeared in her eyes as she stared into the fire. 'And it's the last. That was yesterday evening. This morning I left at first light before he or T-Bone were awake. And I ain't going back.' She fingered the livid mark blighting her face.

Once again Chase attempted to tease out her reason for being up here alone. This time, a wistful cast smoothed out the frown lines marring her complexion. Her hand moved down to the necklace around her neck. The three men noticed it for the first time.

'Danny and me have made a commitment,' she said firmly. 'He gave me this necklace of bear claws as proof that we are now officially engaged to be married.'

'What?' Strawtop could not contain his shock at this unexpected declaration. The blunt exclamation was blurted out. He followed it up by a more practical objection. But it emerged as a biting piece of ridicule. 'That bauble ain't no commitment. You need a proper ring for that.'

Now it was Della's turn to lurch to her feet. Blazing eyes fastened on to the kid. 'How dare you make fun of my betrothal? It might not be the right thing for you, but Danny Maggrie meant every word. And it's what the trappers believe in. They have their own code of conduct up in the mountains. And I for one am more than happy to abide by it.'

A sniff to indicate her contempt for Strawtop's thoughtless remark, a lift of the shoulders and she stamped away to be alone with her thoughts.

'I didn't mean . . . ' But it was too late. The damage had been done.

'You sure are one mossy-horned booby when it comes to dames, ain't you, son?' abraded his partner, shaking his head. The kid lumbered to his feet, hoping to rectify his blunder.

'Leave her be,' his buddy ordered. 'Ain't nothing you can do now. You tell him, Chase.'

But Farlow's thoughts were elsewhere. This was the first mention that the girl's fiancé was one of the notorious Maggrie brothers. The blood drained from his face. This was a complication he did not need. Much as he would have liked to seek out these buzzards and determine if they were the ones who had bushwhacked him and T-Bone, the current job precluded that.

Escorting the ore safely to Ridgeway was the number one priority. Luckily the dim light cast by the camp fire effectively concealed his chagrin.

Ramsey peered at his old friend. 'You hear me, Chase? Tell this lumphead to shackle his loins good while we're on this venture.'

The nudge in his ribs brought Farlow out of his morose contemplation.

'Buck's right, kid. Ain't no future for you in that direction. So buckle up and keep your mind on the job.'

Strawtop grunted and then wandered off to console himself alone, in the opposite direction from the girl.

'I've heard about these irregular rituals they carry out in the remote camps,' Chase commented. 'But a bear claw betrothal is a new one on me.' He felt like telling the girl that she was making a big mistake by getting involved with that clan. But in matters of the heart, nothing would sway a girl in love. And he had more important issues to consider.

'She sure seems adamant about going through with it,' said Ramsey, adding a snort of whiskey to his coffee mug. After all that had been revealed, he figured it was his due. 'Guess you're figuring that we'll have to escort her to Hesperus now.'

Ramsey's less than enthusiastic comment went over Chase's head. He nodded his agreement. His own response was equally devoid of zeal, but for a completely different reason. 'We ain't been given no choice. It's another three days' ride up to Hesperus. No way can we let a lone woman travel that path with grizzlies and mountain lions prowling around. She'd likely get herself lost as well.'

'Looks like your plan to avoid that den of iniquity has gone up in smoke, old buddy,' Buck Ramsey observed in a flat monotone.

Although his devious thoughts were

running more along the lines that it would delay his desire to get hold of their valuable cargo. A growing impatience was concealed with some difficulty. Chase was proving to be a much harder nut to crack than he had figured. And he certainly didn't need Strawtop mooning over some homespun farm girl.

The following two days saw the small party climbing ever higher into the remote wilderness of the upland terrain. They were fast approaching the principal hunting grounds for beaver, fox and deer. Grizzlies were also hunted up here, but only with rifles.

Porcupines, squirrels and chipmunks were a constant sight. Even under these trying circumstances, they offered an uplifting sight, cavorting in the mountain playground. Their startled looks brought hoots of much needed laughter. The animals did not flee from the newcomers, indicating that human interlopers were a distinct rarity within their domain.

Della was particularly enthralled by

their playful antics. She was looking forward to reaching Hesperus and her new affianced. Gabe Strawtop's clumsy remark had been pushed aside, but not forgotten. The girl still maintained an aloof disregard for the kid's fumbling attempts at reconciliation.

Dense ranks of pine and aspen were left behind as the tree cover thinned appreciably. Most of the snow had melted by this time, but small patches remained, a solid indication of the height gained. The highest peaks, however, were still iced over. Many retained their white caps throughout the year.

Extra woollen shirts were worn to counteract the chill. Up here in May, the sun's impact was minimal.

But as the trappers' camp drew closer, a tense mood settled over the three men. Only Della remained upbeat. Strawtop's sporadic efforts to breach the rift with the girl had been politely but firmly rebuffed.

The two men rode in front, wrapped in their own ruminations. Once again,

Ramsey attempted to broach the subject of his buddy needing to make his mark on life before it was too late.

Strawtop had tried to add his bit to the devious twist. But early on, Ramsey had realized that his skills in that department were best left to straight sales pitching. This kind of deception needed guile and cunning that only a close associate could carry off with confidence.

'We're both getting old, partner,' he posited. 'Don't you figure life owes you more than a measly wage working for some wealthy speculator?'

'I've told you before, Buck,' Chase emphasized, arrowing a quizzical look at his associate. 'Self-respect is worth more than all the gold a man can dig up.'

'That attitude sure ain't gonna buy you a secure retirement,' Ramsey scoffed. His attempts to persuade Chase to shift his allegiance were becoming ever more blatant. 'I fancy settling down in a fine house overlooking the ocean in California with a whole pack of servants tending to my every need. Only problem is, I ain't got the necessary readies.'

Chase Farlow was beginning to sense that his old partner might not be the trusted colleague he had expected. This Buck Ramsey appeared to be a different man from the one with whom he had cleaned up Quemado. But Chase was a born optimist by nature. Perhaps his friend was just mouthing off. Age can be a lonely process if you figure that life has not treated you squarely. Calling at Hesperus did not help either. The detour was going to add unwanted time to their journey.

A lot could happen in that time. Prophetic words that were going to haunt him.

Ramsey was arriving at the annoying conclusion that Chase Farlow was one of those few men who were not to be bought off. His partner was still the stalwart of old — honourable and incorruptible, and in Ramsey's view, foolishly naïve.

# 10

## HESPERUS

It was later the following afternoon that a new smell began to impinge itself on to their nasal senses. A sickly odour of decaying animal flesh. It could only have its origins at the trappers' camp. They must be nearing Hesperus. Ten minutes later they crested a rise. And there below was the notorious settlement.

A haphazard amalgamation of grubby tents had been erected in a shallow basin enclosed within a circlet of rocks offering shelter from the biting westerlies. The off-white smear pasted against dull grey rock was bare of adornment and held no enticement for the newcomers. Apart, that is, from Della, whose innocent features glowed in the sunlight.

Only one structure was of a wood

construction. Due to this remote location being above the tree line, the timber had to be carted in. Stacks of pelts lay close by, awaiting storage in the barn prior to the trek north up to the Green River rendezvous. This was a twice yearly meeting that was much anticipated. Trappers from all sections of the mountain country gathered to sell their wares to traders from the east.

The heyday of the rendezvous had long since passed. But the mountain men who still continued this lonely existence enjoyed the party atmosphere that prevailed. Friends looked forward to meeting up with those not seen for long periods. Between the bouts of drinking, fighting, games and contests, the serious business of trading was carried on. And judging by the large collection of drying hides that littered the camp, the next rendezvous could be imminent.

The smell of scraped animal hides together with bits discarded hung heavy over the camp. On sighting the newcomers, all work stopped. Strangers were a distinct rarity in Hesperus. Few people voluntarily strayed this far into the wild uplands of the Sierra Negras. As the small column drew closer, it was clear that the inhabitants of the camp were mostly clad in furs due to the cold climate.

Lighter buckskins would not be worn for at least another month. Men and women were barely distinguishable. All had long straggly hair. Deep furrows occasioned by the harsh outdoor life scored their ebony, dirt-streaked faces.

Strawtop winced. Was this how Della Speinkampf would look in another six months? Surely a girl of her upbringing deserved better than what he now witnessed. The kid felt like voicing his concerns. But already they were entering the outskirts of the camp. The people parted. Nobody smiled. Indeed, many of the upturned faces bore hostile expressions. A low murmuring could not help but unsettle the intruders.

Strawtop voiced their joint apprehension. 'These guys don't exactly seem welcoming, do they?' He did not expect a reply to the tremulous aside. Only Della seemed oblivious to the less than cordial reception. Her eyes scanned the burgeoning throng searching for her fiancé.

Some of the more inquisitive inhabitants stepped forward to obtain a closer peek at the heavily laden mules. Nerves already showing, Strawtop knocked a reaching hand away from the covered strong boxes. A low growl akin to that from a wounded beast grumbled in the offender's throat.

'Keep a lid on that temper, kid,' rasped Farlow angrily through the side of his mouth. 'Do you want us to be shot down before we've even had a chance to introduce ourselves? Handling these varmints needs tact and diplomacy.'

'Chase is right,' agreed Ramsey. 'We don't stand a chance if'n these fellas take a dislike to us.'

The tense stand-off was punctured when a dark-haired young guy pushed through the crowd. A huge smile was plastered over his face.

'Della! Is that you?' he exclaimed, grabbing all the attention. 'Didn't reckon I'd be seeing you until our next meeting at Hermosa in a couple of weeks.'

The girl leapt off her horse and fell into the man's arms. 'Oh, Danny,' she burbled, unable to contain her tears. 'Am I glad to see you.' They kissed in front of the whole assembly, an action that engendered a round of applause and much hallooing.

Finally breaking apart, Danny Maggrie posed the obvious question. 'What are you doing up here so soon after we last met? Has something happened?'

More tears flowed down the girl's cheeks. 'It's Pa,' she sobbed. 'He found out we were seeing each other. We had an almighty row and he hit me.' She then revealed the discoloured bruise. Gasps erupted from the onlookers. It sure was a shiner. 'So the next morning I lit out and came up here. These gentlemen were good enough to make sure I reached Hesperus safely.'

Once again, the eyes of the gathering swung back to the three mounted men and their pack mules. Danny's smile dissolved as his narrowed gaze fastened on to the handsome visage of Gabe Strawtop. They were of a similar age. Danny immediately sensed the presence of a rival suitor. It was written as clear as day across the newcomer's scowling regard.

Three other men elbowed their way through the crowd to join the younger Maggrie. They were clearly held in esteem by the other trappers as they spread out on either side of him. All wore the ragged apparel supplied by their trapped prey. Even down to the thick hide boots.

The oldest was Wolf, who was chewing on a haunch of venison. He was the only one of the four brothers who sported a store-bought hat. Yet even that had lost all its shape. His younger twin brothers, Fester and Silas, both wore coonskin caps and were clutching Sharps breech loading rifles to their chests. Cooper five-shot pistols were provocatively displayed in their belts.

Their bulging eyes were drawn to the mules. Fester slavered greedily. He had always claimed that gold had a distinctive smell.

Hostility and confrontation emanated from every pore of the three men.

Buck Ramsey leaned across to his old partner, murmuring out of the side of his mouth, 'Didn't you say one of them bushwhackers was shot?' A barely noticeable flick of the head indicated the dirty bandage swathing Silas Maggrie's head. A bullet wound on one side and the scalloped ear on the other.

Chase nodded. His whispered reply was meant for no other ears. 'But all I saw was a fleeting shadow. And I'd never recognize those two jaspers I arrested in Durango. We need to tread carefully if'n we're to leave this dump with our own hides intact.'

Silas was likewise eyeing the tall figure of the ex-marshal. His face screwed up in thought. He had seen the guy some place before. But for the life of him, he couldn't recall where. He shrugged off the notion. It would come to him before too long. Had he realized that scratching his damaged ear was the clue, his manner would not have been so blasé.

It was Danny Maggrie who interrupted the covert muttering among the newcomers, enunciating the general feeling of those present.

'Much obliged for delivering my gal up here, gents.' He paused, a mirthless smile, cold and unbending encompassing the three newcomers. 'Now it's time to leave.'

The silence that descended over the encampment was palpable. Men waited expectantly for something to happen. Three against innumerable opponents did not auger well for Chase Farlow and his associates, should they choose to ignore Danny Maggrie's blunt directive.

It was Della who attempted to pour oil on the troubled waters as she stepped forward to offer her support.

'These men didn't have to come up here, Danny,' she contended. 'They have gone out of their way to escort me. And the day is well gone. So why not let them stay the night? I'm sure you boys don't begrudge them a place to set down and rest up.'

Danny considered the appeal. A lurid smirk creased his face. His arm encircled Della's waist. Then he pulled her close and roughly caressed her soft body. Eager hands avidly sought out those intimate spots a man fashions in his dreams. It was all a deliberate ploy to needle the suspected contender for his fiancée's affections. Throughout the shameful display, a mocking disregard for Della's feelings was coupled with the deliberate challenge for Strawtop to intervene.

Ramsey immediately perceived young Maggrie's intentions. Accordingly, he nudged his horse in front of his young partner, a surreptitious hand staying any recklessly foolish comeback. He was only just in time.

Gabe's tormented stare was black as a thunder cloud.

Della was startled by the sudden assault on her person. Was this how married couples behaved up here in the wilds? It sure wasn't how she had been brought up. Both her parents had been restrained and discreet in displaying their affections.

The unwelcome pawing was quickly brought to a halt when she forcibly pulled away. This was not the Danny Maggrie she had come to admire. Yet she still accorded him the benefit of the doubt. Perhaps he was just showing off to his brothers. Or was it jealousy that had made him act like a cocky rooster? Della was well aware that Gabe Strawtop was also holding a torch for her.

And it wasn't every day that a girl had two men squabbling over her. Indeed it had never happened before. After she had given it some more thought, the experience was actually quite pleasant.

'Isn't it you that I've come up here to marry?' she persisted, squaring off while fingering the necklace of bear claws. 'Let them stay the night. Then tomorrow we'll be married. I've even brought my own dress especially for the occasion. It was Ma's. And I've been saving it just for you.'

The sudden notion that Danny was to become a married man brought a round of cheering with hats flung into the air. He was now the centre of attention and felt important. Getting hitched would make him a man in the eyes of the camp rather than merely his brothers' younger kin to be pushed around at will.

Preening and posturing like a proud peacock, he strutted up and down, allowing men and their women to congratulate him.

While this was going on, Fester had sidled up behind Della. His hands reached around and grabbed her breasts. Ever since the newcomers had arrived, lustful eyes had been devouring this winsome creature. It was abundantly clear that beneath the baggy trail duds was a shapely woman with all the right bits to match.

Della screamed.

'Aaaaaagh!' she wailed, struggling desperately to free herself. 'Please Danny, help me! Get this filthy animal off me.'

But it was Gabe Strawtop who came to her rescue. Before Ramsey could intervene, the kid had leapt off his horse. A scything right hook smashed into the elder Maggrie's cheek. The assailant was sent staggering back. He tumbled to the floor. Gabe stood over him, breathing deeply. He was more than ready to continue the beating should it be required.

Fester grabbed for his pistol. But a

blunt order to desist stayed the instinctive retaliation. It had come from Danny Maggrie. 'You asked for that, Fester. Della is my gal, and don't you forget it.'

His cowed brother wiped a streak of blood from his cut cheek. Although the older by five years, he nevertheless backed off under the glowering stare of his younger kin. But his hate-filled eyes were reserved for the hovering figure of Gabe Strawtop.

'You ain't heard the last of this, mister,' he growled.

'Anytime, dog-breath,' countered the irate Strawtop, bunching his fists.

Fester snarled, then turned his wrath on his younger kin. 'You seem to be forgetting that it's a family tradition, boy,' he rasped. 'Share and share alike. And that means everything' — he leered at his other brothers — 'including women. Ain't that the god-damned truth, boys?'

There was no dispute from any of the watching throng. The camp shared everything. It was how they were able to survive amidst the harsh terrain. Yet on this occasion, Danny Maggrie intended to break with that customary practice.

'Well, that sure ain't gonna extend to my wife,' he reiterated vehemently. 'So get that into your thick skulls. All of you!' Grumbling remonstrations followed. But they soon fizzled out. This was neither the time nor place to argue amongst themselves.

But the sly look on Fester Maggrie's ugly visage hinted that his younger brother was not going to escape retribution for this public humiliation. Stumbling to his feet, he stroked a sleeve across his mashed lips, then disappeared amongst the ragged swathe of humanity.

Satisfied to have made a firm point, Danny then swung back to address the edgy figure of Gabe Strawtop.

'I'm obliged for your intervention, mister. You can stay the night but keep away from the camp.' The appreciative response to Strawtop's intercession was quickly discarded as a hard-boiled warning was delivered. 'And if'n I catch you anywhere near my wife, you're a dead man, savvy?'

The two cocky tearaways held each other's gaze, neither flinching. Strawtop remained silent.

But he had gotten the message and Buck Ramsey firmly intended that he would abide by it. It was Ramsey who brought the tense stand-off to a neutral, if not entirely satisfactory, conclusion. He nudged his horse between the two young hotheads.

'We'll make sure he abides by your wishes, mister.'

'You do that,' rapped Danny Maggrie.

Ramsey shot a warning look at his partner before quickly hustling him away. Chase followed, hissing out a silent curse. A partner who harboured romantic visions for a betrothed woman was a problem he could well do without. Hassles were building up too darned fast for his liking.

As both parties accepted the tentative truce, the gathering slowly broke up. Various factions among the trappers moved away, eager to discuss the recent events. Most important as far as the men were concerned was that the morrow would herald an almighty drinking session that would last for at least two days. Weddings according to mountain community traditions happened rarely. So this was a good excuse to have a good time.

The women quickly commandeered Della, hustling her into their communal tent. They were all eager to see the dress and get the girl decked out in her finery in preparation for the big day. The girl turned one last time. The smile she aimed in Gabe Strawtop's direction was like a shining beacon amidst the grim squalor of the trappers' camp. It made his rash intervention on the girl's behalf worth every nugget of gold they were toting.

Chase led them off to a level sward behind some rocks which would isolate them from the racket expected from the coming prenuptial shindig. He and Buck built a fire and set down the skillet and coffee pot.

Although removed from the camp, there was to be little sleep for either faction that night. The trappers were intent on ensuring that Danny's last night as a single man was celebrated in time-honoured fashion. Jugs of strong moonshine together with home-brewed beer were opened and liberally consumed by one and all. Singing and dancing continued well into the early hours.

None of this bothered Buck Ramsey. His mind was busily figuring out a plan of action to purloin the gold without harming his old partner.

He was now convinced that Chase would not go along with the proposed heist. Nevertheless, if'n his old buddy chose to resist, Buck Ramsey reckoned he would not hesitate to chop him down. It went against his instincts, but acquisition of the gold had to overrule their past friendship.

Gabe Strawtop spent most of the time watching the ever more frenetic antics of the cavorting revellers. He kept asking himself the same question over and over. Why had Della rejected him in favour of some half-witted jackass? His nerves were stretched to breaking point wondering how she was faring down there in the den of iniquity. Equally as bad was the fear that Fester Maggrie might well try his hand again once he'd filled up on moonshine.

Gabe had almost convinced himself to go down there and rescue the poor girl when Buck Ramsey jerked him back to the reality of their situation.

'Ain't I already told you to forget that dame, Gabe? She came up here of her own free will. Nobody forced her hand, unless you count that Bible-bashing father.' Ramsey's tone was blunt and unequivocal.

'Concentrate your thoughts on how you and me are going to get the drop on Farlow. My patience is running on thin air. Get me?'

'Sure, sure, Buck. It's just that . . . '
The kid's gaze shifted once more towards the whooping saturnalia in Hesperus.

'No buts!' snapped Ramsey, jabbing a finger at his partner. 'You're either with me or agin me. Now what's it to be?'

'Of course I'm in, Buck. You know that.'

'Then get some sleep. We need to make our move tomorrow.'

Reluctantly, Strawtop dragged himself away. But sleep was a long time coming. The features of Della Speinkampf's angelic face continued to haunt his dreams, the dulcet tone of her soft voice gnawing away at his resolve.

It was sometime later as the first streaks of dawn were clawing aside the frigid gloom of night that he was suddenly jerked awake. He sat up. Something had disturbed him. But for the moment he couldn't figure out what it was. Then it came again.

A spine-tingling shriek ripped apart

the all too brief respite of sleep. And it was coming from the tented enclave. He sat up, suddenly wide awake. That was no drunken howl of merriment. It was a scream of terror that he had heard before.

Della was in trouble.

Shrugging off his blanket, the kid quickly shucked into his boots and snatched up his gun belt. His buddies slept on, completely oblivious to the ugly drama about to be played out.

# 11

## RESCUE AT DAWN

Although Fester Maggrie had appeared to keep up with the drink consumed by his brothers, he had deliberately held back. Erotic visions conjured up by his inept groping of Della Speinkampf were impossible to ignore. And the more he thought about that delectable piece of forbidden fruit, the more he wanted a substantial bite of the apple. Nobody in Hesperus could match her for looks and freshness.

Women quickly lost their initial magnetism, that sparkling bloom of novelty, once the hard life of catering for the trapping community set in. Such would be the inevitable lot of his young brother's betrothed soon enough. In consequence, Fester intended to seek out a piece of the action early on now that Danny had decided to go against family tradition.

He nudged the boy in the ribs. A burbled grunt was his sole response. The younger Maggrie was well and truly soused, just as Fester had intended. It hadn't taken much. Danny was not as used to hard liquor in the same quantities as his older brothers. A leery smirk creased Fester's visage. He crawled out of the tent and peered across to the large awning, strung between poles over on the far side of the camp. That was where he knew Della would be sleeping.

A rooster crowed in the fowl enclosure heralding the imminent arrival of first light. This did not worry Fester. The women had drunk their fill just like their men-folk. And if'n that was also the case with Della Speinkampf, so much the better. It would save him having to keep her quiet while he sampled the goods.

The thought of those lithe and supple limbs made his loins tingle. He could barely contain his ardour. One last check that his brothers were comatose. Then he quietly slipped across to the awning. He was well aware that a potential bride was accorded the privilege of separate sleeping quarters on her final night of freedom. A thick woollen blanket separated her from the others who were snoring loud enough to raise the canvas roof.

Fester slid into the booth, feverishly unbuckling his pants. He could hardly wait to get started.

Oblivious to the threatened assault looming over her, Della was lying on her back. A loose arm cradled her head. Fester ogled the supine form, her titian locks spread across the pillow. His initial supposition regarding the girl's allure had been amply rewarded. Now he was about to enjoy the delights on offer.

Della had declined the earlier invitation by the camp women to indulge in their celebratory imbibing. If her austere father had taught her anything, it was most definitely the evils occasioned by the demon drink. She had lain awake for a long time after her wedding attendants had succumbed to its insensible effects.

Listening to the tales relayed by her new companions made the girl increasingly mindful that she had made the biggest mistake of her life in coming up here. Now that she knew the score, life back on the farm assumed the semblance of an idyllic haven compared with the hell that was Hesperus.

Tomorrow, Danny Maggrie would claim his due. And his odious brothers would be itching to claim their rightful concession according to the family tradition. Danny may have denied his kin the privileged entitlement. But Della had little faith that such a resistance could be maintained indefinitely. Then she would become like one of these unsightly harridans, forced to adopt the worn-out lugubrious lifestyle of a trapper's wife.

Feeling abjectly sorry for herself,

Della had cried herself to sleep. When Fester loomed over her, the limpid smile playing across the girl's smooth features implied a yearning invitation on her part for the trapper's attention. In truth, she was dreaming about being rescued from this demonic torment by Gabe Strawtop. How could she have been so taken in by Danny Maggrie's coarse charm?

It was the fumbling beneath her buckskinned quilt that brought her awake. At first, she could not figure out what was taking place. Had one of the camp dogs sneaked into her sleeping quarters in search of warmth? But this was no canine snuggling. A hand was pawing at her nightgown, rough and accompanied by a guttural wheezing redolent of male sweat.

Had Danny decided that he could not wait for the morrow to exercise his marital rights? No, that couldn't be. This intruder was much heavier. The direful truth hit her between the eyes. It was Fester Maggrie intent on continuing his lustful predilection. Her mouth opened to scream. But her assailant had figured on such a move. A gnarled paw quickly curtailed the anguished holler while his other continued to force her legs apart.

Sheer panic gripped the girl's innards. Unless she did something, her maidenhood was going to be violated in the most appalling way. There was only one course of action open to her.

She bit down on to an exposed finger, drawing blood together with a sharp howl of pain from the injured man. Instinctively, Fester removed his hand, giving Della the opportunity to exercise her lungs.

She screamed loudly, venting her spleen by clawing at her attacker's face. Sharp nails raked bloody lines down the coarse leathery skin.

'Gabe! Gabe!' she yelled, wriggling away from the angry rapist.

Although Maggrie was initially taken aback by this sudden resistance, he soon recovered. No hick farm girl was going to be denied to him. He snarled, roughly grabbing her to him. But Della was now wide awake. Not having consumed any alcohol gave her an edge she hoped would thwart the odious creature's hideous depredation.

Some of the women on the far side of the makeshift wall were stirring. Brains still dulled by strong drink, they were, however, ignorant of what was happening.

Over on the far side of the camp, somebody called out a slurred inquiry as to the racket that had disturbed his slumber.

Maggrie knew that he had to act quickly. A swinging hand rose to deliver a stunning blow that would irreversibly curb the girl's feeble attempts to frustrate his ardent passion.

It never landed. Another hand grabbed the trapper's arm, dragging him off the struggling female.

'What in thunderation is going on?' snapped Maggrie, who had been taken completely by surprise. 'Who are you?'

159

In the dim light, the human features were devoid of substance.

'I'm the one who's gonna kill you,' came back the blunt response. It was Gabe Strawtop. At the same time he turned to Della. 'Get over to our camp, pronto!'

Instantly recognizing the welcome voice of her paladin, the girl scrambled away from the dangerous predator.

'You!' exclaimed Maggrie. 'I ought to have settled your hash before I came over here. My mistake. But I won't make another.'

His uninjured hand grabbed for the knife always kept in a boot sheath. In seconds it was palmed. The razor-edged blade flashed as he made to rip his assailant's guts out. Strawtop was ready and saw the deadly manoeuvre coming. He pushed himself back just in time as the lethal slash cut through his shirt. Luckily it only nicked his skin.

A gun appeared in the kid's hand. This was no time for dithering. The hammer snapped back, the trigger finger tightening. A momentary hesitation as Maggrie gathered himself for another lunge. Flashing through Strawtop's brain was the fleeting notion that he was about to shoot down his first human assailant.

But that's all it was, a transitory thought. Then the gun exploded, hot lead delivering its deadly charge. Maggrie grunted as the slug punched him back through the blanket wall. A series of anguished groans informed the shooter that it was not a killing shot. But Fester Maggrie would certainly not be pursuing his attacker.

Gabe backed off, panning the revolver from side to side as men slowly stumbled out of their pits. Shouts that disturb drink-induced sleep are irritating, but can be shrugged off. Not gunfire. Calls as to the cause of the shooting echoed across the camp site.

An owl hooted, also disturbed by the abnormal clamour. Dogs barked, adding to the confusion. The overbearing effects of the alcoholic haze only served to increase the mayhem.

Chase and his partner had also been awakened. They were already on their feet when Della Speinkampf hustled into view, followed soon after by Strawtop.

'What have you been up to?' rapped the angry voice of Buck Ramsey. 'Couldn't keep your dirty hands to yourself? Is that it?' He was riled up and ready to deliver his own punitive chastisement. 'What did I tell you about leaving her alone?'

It was Della who succinctly apprised the two older men of Gabe's fortuitous intervention on her behalf. From the bubbling uproar in Hesperus, it was clear that a swift exit was now their only course of action. This was no time for analysing the pros and cons of the young man's blunt interference. They needed to skedaddle, rapido.

Luckily, the animals were already packed in readiness for an early start. All that was needed was to saddle up the horses. But with four of them, somebody would have to ride double. Gabe immediately offered to take Della on his mount. Sheer relief at having escaped the torment of the camp, she fell into the kid's arms. He hugged her tight. Yet even he knew that this was no time for dawdling.

The fire was doused and within minutes, the small party were once again heading back the way they had come. The ensuing confusion among the trappers would give them a good start.

Chase led the way. The false dawn provided sufficient light to enable them to set a brisk pace. The original plan of heading over the Sierra Negras to Ridgeway was now abandoned. Chase knew that he would have to deliver the girl back to her father down on the farm. No way was he coming back up this way again.

He was also well aware that the betrothed trapper would not take this assault on their camp lying down. According to Gabe, Fester Maggrie was out of the reckoning. But Danny and his other brothers would want revenge for this blatant challenge to their reputation and standing in the community. Stealing a man's woman from under his very nose would need unequivocal retribution otherwise Danny would become a laughing stock among his peers.

Chase knew full well that with a girl riding double the inevitable confrontation was likely to come all too soon. He dropped back to have words with Ramsey.

His partner was struggling to contain his anger. Things were rapidly spiralling out of his control. Although he was still intent on getting his hands on the gold. The girl's unwelcome inclusion in his plans for a second time was an aggravation he would have to bear. Along with Chase, he harboured a loathing for those who treated women like chattels. Having taken account of the Maggrie brothers and their ilk at Hesperus, Buck was loath to cast her back into such a hell's kitchen.

With some effort, he managed to keep his thoughts regarding the upset to his devious plan under wraps when Chase dropped back to voice his thoughts about their unexpected predicament.

'Those jaspers will be on our trail soon as they've figured out what happened,' he remarked in a fractious tone. 'And they'll be wanting our blood and the girl's surrender. I for one ain't willing for that to happen.'

He fixed a gimlet eye on his associate, automatically assuming that Ramsey would concur with that viewpoint.

'Me neither,' Ramsey agreed. 'So what's the plan?'

'With the girl riding double, they'll likely catch us up by noon.' Ramsey nodded. 'So we need to find a good place to set up an ambush. And I've been thinking.' He paused, offering his buddy a half smile. 'Remember Chancellorsville back in '63?'

Ramsey's wary regard broadened

into a beaming smile. The incident referred to leapt to the forefront of his thoughts as he continued Chase's line of thought. 'The Rebs had us on the run. They would have cut us down as well if'n you hadn't spotted that ravine.'

Chase finished the all too familiar story. 'We could do the same thing here if'n we find a similar formation. You and Gabe on one side, with me on the other.'

'Catch them in a crossfire,' Ramsey said, enthused by his partner's fervour. 'It worked like a charm then. No reason why we can't achieve the same result today.'

Chancellorsville had been an ignominious setback for the Union forces. But Sergeant Chase Farlow's initiative had snatched a small victory from the jaws of defeat. Gabe was included in the plan, which he eagerly endorsed.

Although his main concern was to deliver Della safely back to the farm. Unlike his partner, the lifting of the gold had now become a secondary issue.

From that moment, all their attention was focused on the landscape and searching for an ideal place to resurrect that brief but noteworthy wartime incident. It was around midday that Chase found the ideal spot for which he had been seeking. The trail passed through a narrow rift with plenty of cover on each side. He signalled a halt. 'This looks like the place to get the drop on those skunks,' he said to Buck.

'Me and you can range ourselves over yonder behind those rocks,' Ramsey concurred. 'Gabe can look after the girl on this side.'

And so it was agreed. There was no knowing when the pursuers would arrive. But it was bound to be within the next hour. Once the horses and pack mules were hobbled securely out of sight, Chase made sure that Strawtop was under strict instructions to obey orders.

'Got that, kid?' he insisted with

vigour. 'No premature shooting until I give the signal.'

Ensconced behind their respective covering of boulders, the four of them settled down to await the arrival of the Maggries and whomsoever they could persuade to accompany them.

# 12

## INCIDENT AT
## PANDORA'S GORGE

Ten minutes later, Chase noticed a plume of smoke rising from behind the rocks concealing Strawtop and the girl. The still air gave it the appearance of a length of white rope.

'Is that turkey intent on causing more darned trouble?' he railed at his sidekick. 'That smoke can easily be spotted for miles around. If'n he carries on like this, it'll be us receiving a surprise present up our butts.'

He squinted against the noonday sun, probing their back trail for any sign that the hunters were getting close. Luckily the coast appeared to be clear.

It was Ramsey who vented his spleen against the negligent youth. He had little doubt that the kid was trying out the chat-up lines with which he had been primed by his more experienced colleague. But this was neither the time nor the place for flirtatious discourse. Their lives were at stake here.

He shouted across the intervening gap. The virulent growl quickly found the kid raising his head above the parapet.

'Douse that cigar butt pronto, you darned fool,' came the stern rebuke. 'Do you want to hand those critters a message giving away our plans?'

Strawtop's face turned a bright red. He bit back an acrid response. Just as mortifying as the implied carelessness was his loss of prestige in Della Speinkampf's eyes. Nevertheless, he immediately complied with the blunt order while thinking up some excuse to nullify his partner's brusque put-down.

Not wanting his partner to be too discomfited, Ramsey called back in a more conciliatory tone. 'Guess you weren't thinking straight, boy. It happens to us all in times of stress.'

'You shouldn't be going so easy on that bungling greenhorn,' Chase censured his partner. 'Actions like that cost lives.'

Ramsey shrugged but said nothing. His gaze was focused back along the trail. But his mind was still working out how to get the drop on his associate and lift that all-important booty. Chase was a little lower down with his back to the conniving charlatan. Glinting eyes sighted along the barrel of his rifle, a finger playing with the trigger. It would be so easy. Just one shot and the gold would be his.

Burning eyes narrowed to thin slits. One shot. The finger tightened . . . then slackened off. Reason overruled Ramsey's intense need to acquire the loot. He needed the ex-marshal to be rid of those darned Maggries. Once they had been dealt with, that would be the moment to make his move.

Yet deep within his subliminal values was another voice urging him to desist. This guy was his oldest friend. They went back a long way, had fought in the bloody conflict of the Civil War. How could such reprehensible thoughts be holding sway? Then the red mist descended once again as the lure of easy riches brushed aside the arguments of conscience.

The battle betwixt good and evil was thrust aside as Chase raised his arm, pointing along the trail to a cloud of dust rising above the tree line.

'Here they come, boys,' he called out. 'Make every shot count. But wait on my signal to get this shindig up and running.'

A few minutes later, a dozen riders hove into view. In the lead was the burly figure of Wolf Maggrie with his brother Danny by his side. Behind him rode Silas, the bandage swathing his head clearly visible. A host of other trappers had also elected to join the manhunt. All were heavily armed with rifles and pistols clearly on display. The narrowing trail through Pandora's Gorge forced the galloping band down to a walk.

On they came, completely oblivious to the trap into which they were heading like rats to the slaughter.

Only when they were well within rifle range and unable to turn round freely did Chase Farlow open fire. A boisterous holler of tense exhilaration burst from his pent-up lungs. Within seconds, bullets were flying everywhere. Smoke from the three long guns lifted into the still air. The peace and tranquillity of Pandora's Gorge was ripped apart in dramatic fashion.

A flock of buzzards quickly lifted into the sky, frightened by the sudden shattering of their silent world.

Two of the unwitting trappers immediately bit the dust, caught in the lethal crossfire. Pandemonium erupted as horses reared up on hind legs, desperately trying to escape the lethal barrage raining down on them. The pure instinct for survival now kicked in as Wolf Maggrie urged his fellows to seek cover. Bullets kicked sand near their feet as the remaining trappers leapt out of the saddle, frantically scrambling behind any cover available.

Another rider bit the dust before he could scramble for safety.

Amidst the deadly mayhem, three horses had also been chopped down. Panic-stricken, the other riderless animals galloped off back up the trail, eager to distance themselves from the life and death struggle.

The victims of the deadly contest now began to return fire. But they were at a distinct disadvantage, being lower down than their assailants amidst a collection of small rocks that barely afforded any serious cover.

Chase Farlow had chosen his position well. One of the trappers, stuck behind a dead horse, attempted to run across the level sward to join his buddies. He made it halfway before Strawtop cut him down.

'Yahooooo!' roared the gleeful kid. 'And another one goes down! See that, Buck? Ain't this some'n else?'

Farlow scowled. This was no Sunday

school picnic. And that kid was becoming a mite too keen on lethal gunplay. He would need watching when they came out of this fracas . . . just like his partner.

Danny Maggrie was screaming abuse at the three bushwhackers.

'We'll get you bunch of rats,' he yelled out. 'No thieving skunks are gonna get the better of a Maggrie by stealing his dame. You hear that, pisspot? I'm gonna eat you alive.' His rabid comments were clearly aimed at Gabe Strawtop.

The kid laughingly poured scorn on the impotent threats. 'You ain't had much luck so far, maggothead.' A scornful guffaw accompanied the insulting dub. 'Della's with me now. She don't want nothing to do with an ugly worm like you.'

He felt a firm grip on his arm. Turning round, Della gave him the warmest of smiles that set his heart apounding. Unhooking the bear tooth necklace from around her neck, she passed it to him, then nodded towards the cowering trappers. The intimation was clear. Gabe smiled back, squeezing her hand. He took hold of the bauble and keeping under cover, slung it high overhead so that it landed in the open.

'You gotten the message?' he bawled. 'This is from Della. Now crawl back where you came from. Otherwise you'll all end up as crow bait.'

For a moment, the gunfire eased as the trappers considered their position. Wolf knew that they were effectively pinned down. There was no way forwards. Their horses had stampeded. And the attackers held the high ground. Their situation was bleak. An assault across open ground would be suicidal.

Danny Maggrie had no such reservations. His blinkered train of thought urged just such a course of action.

Wolf grabbed his brother firmly by the arm.

'Don't be a darned idiot,' he snapped. 'Go out there now and we'll all be shot down like dogs.' He tried shaking some much needed sense into the crazy kid. 'Back off and we can catch them later. And at our own bidding. But first we need to think it out and go after our mounts.'

'He's right, boy,' Silas concurred with his elder brother. It had suddenly come to him where he had previously encountered the leader of this bunch. 'And I'm just as eager as you to see them skunks in hell.' A meaningful finger tapped the blood-stained bandage.

The pressing insistence of his two brothers eventually penetrated Danny's addled brain.

'OK, we'll do it your way,' he said, forcing his seething brain to calm down. 'Just so long as I get to deal with that slimy rat who's tricked Della.'

'It's the right way,' Silas interjected in support of his elder brother. 'And don't you fret none, Danny boy. We'll get them.'

'OK, mister,' Wolf called out in a suitably contrite voice. 'You win. We're giving up the chase. You fellas are much too slick for the likes of us. How's about letting us back off? Our horses have disappeared. And it'll take hours to round them up. So we can't follow you . . . What do you say?'

Chase considered the proposition. They had made their point. The trappers had been well and truly bested. No point, therefore, in prolonging the conflict unnecessarily.

'It's a deal, Maggrie,' he replied. 'But we'll be watching you boys like hawks until you've disappeared round Indian's Head Butte over yonder.'

Cautiously, the remaining trappers emerged from their flimsy cover and began plodding back up the trail. Two of them needed help, having sustained minor gunshot wounds. Danny kept looking back towards the hidden attackers. The scowling expression was intended to convey the notion that as far as he was concerned, this conflict was far from over.

Only when he was sure that the trappers had left the field of conflict did

Chase give the order to mount up and continue their journey.

For the rest of the afternoon, they kept a constant watch on their back trail to ensure the trappers were not following. Gabe even volunteered to act as a rear guard. He caught the others up at the point where the trail split. The kid's return was what Buck Ramsey had been waiting for. Now was the moment to make their move.

Chase had dismounted to have a closer look at the steepening section that led down through the columbine carpet to Coal Bank Pass more than two thousand feet below. He was considering whether to make camp before attempting the acclivitous descent. Climbing up was always a heap easier when tackling rough stony ground. On the down grade, a horse could easily slip and throw its rider. Much of the descent would, therefore, have to be done on foot.

Chase was about to turn round and make the announcement when the distinct click of a gun being cocked assaulted his sharp senses. He froze in mid-stride. Without turning round, he knew exactly what was happening.

'I was wondering when you were gonna make your move, Buck,' he remarked forlornly.

The comment was spiked with disappointment. He had desperately wanted to give his old partner the benefit of the doubt. 'Just goes to show. You never can trust anyone where gold is involved. I assume that's what this is all about?'

'I wanted you to come in with us, Chase. Still do.' Ramsey was almost pleading with his associate to back their skulduggery. 'You don't owe that guy anything. We can disappear into the mountains. Head for California. I hear it's warm and sunny all year round over there. We could all live like kings. There's more than enough loot to keep us in clover for the rest of our lives.'

Chase gave the plea a slow shake of the head. 'All my life I've tried to do the right thing. That's what makes getting up in the morning worthwhile. What you're suggesting goes against the grain.' He stepped forward a pace, hand outstretched. 'Now give me the gun, Buck.'

'Damn your high and mighty principles,' snapped Ramsey, his body stiffening. 'And keep your distance. I'm taking that gold, with or without your help. And I'll shoot if'n you give me any trouble.'

'That's a darned shame,' replied Chase with genuine sadness. 'I had you down for a true friend, a guy that I could trust.' His eyes assumed a steely glare. 'Seems I was wrong. You're nought but a common thief.'

Ramsey gritted his teeth, but kept his rising temper. 'Get his gun, Gabe. We ain't got time for no more idle jawing.'

Strawtop was standing behind his partner. His left arm was slung around the shoulders of his beloved. In his right was a fully cocked Colt .45. And it was pointing at Ramsey. 'Guess I can't do that, Buck. Now you holster that gun and shuck your belt slow and easy.'

Now it was Ramsey's turn to freeze. 'What you playing at, boy?' exclaimed the startled Judas. 'Do you want the whole caboodle all for yourself, is that it?'

'I've been thinking long and hard about this over the last couple of days.' Although Strawtop's voice trembled now that the confrontation was finally out in the open, his gun hand remained steady as a rock. 'And since meeting Della, I want to settle down with her and live an honest life. Her pa is getting old. And I want nothing more than to help run the spread with a good woman by my side. The gold don't mean nothing to me anymore.'

Chase was as startled by this sudden change in circumstances as his double-crossing old comrade.

'What you are aiming to do is all wrong,' the kid iterated. 'Now drop that gun! I've killed once today. I don't want another shooting on my conscience.

But I will pull this trigger if'n that's what it takes.'

Chase quickly recovered his composure by stepping briskly forwards to remove the revolver from Ramsey's hand, followed by the rifle from his saddle boot. Then, without any further preamble he ordered Ramsey to leave.

'Take the trail back to Silverton,' he rasped with barely controlled anger. 'And don't let me see hide nor hair of you again.'

Ramsey was left to scowl impotently. He could do nothing to salvage his lost initiative with two guns pointing his way. Without saying another word, he spurred off down the left-hand fork in the trail.

After watching the turncoat disappear around a bend in the trail, it was some minutes before anybody spoke. The swift reversal of circumstances had taken them all by surprise in different ways. Chase had harboured misgivings about his old partner that had proved to have substance. And young Gabe

Strawtop changing sides was equally astonishing. The kid certainly appeared to be genuinely remorseful.

It was left for Della to pose the all-important question after realizing the enormity of what he and Buck Ramsey had been planning all along.

'Did you mean what you said, Gabe?' Della Speinkampf inquired tentatively. 'You've betrayed your partner claiming it was all for me. I have to be sure that what you're saying is for real and not some spur-of-the-moment decision that you will live to regret. My father is not going to be easy to convince of your sincerity. Unless you are a regular church-goer and can quote passages from the Bible, he'll look on you almost as an agent of the Devil.'

'I can vouch for that, boy,' interrupted Chase. 'Begging your pardon, Della, but he ain't the easiest of men to admire.'

Della did not disagree as her earnest expression searched Strawtop's handsome visage for a wavering sign of vacillation. There was none.

'Believe me, Della,' he exclaimed fervently. 'I meant every last word. And I'll make it my business to convince your pa that I'm the guy for you.'

'You've convinced me,' she replied. 'But what about Mr Farlow? It's him you and your associate were planning to rob. He has to have the final say.' The two young people looked at the old lawdog nervously, assessing his reaction to Strawtop's apparent change of heart.

Chase maintained a stoically indifferent expression as he considered the dilemma now facing him. By rights he ought to take the kid in as an accessory to the intended robbery. On the other hand, the boy had scuttled his partner's heinous scheme. It was Gabe Strawtop's next move that sealed his decision. The boy handed over his revolver butt first to prove that his contrition was genuine.

Chase accepted the gun. Nevertheless, he still kept the kid on tenterhooks. Strawtop had intended to steal the gold. Only the unexpected arrival of

Della Speinkampf on the scene had changed his mind. Should he put the kid under arrest and hand him over to the authorities when they reached Durango? It was a quandary that was not easy to resolve.

But resolve it he did. After what seemed like a month of high noons, the stony features finally relaxed as he returned the kid's gun. The grim regard, however, still held Strawtop in a rigid embrace. A low-voiced warning left the kid in no doubt where he stood.

'But if'n I ever hear that you've proved me and Della wrong, I'll make it my business to hunt you down.'

'Don't worry, boss, I'm a changed man,' Strawtop enthused. 'And I have Della to thank for that. She's made me see the error of my ways. Ain't no way I'm gonna toss that away.'

Della's face lit up as she hugged him close. 'Then let's get down to the farm and make our play together. Pa will surely see the light when he hears from me what you've done.'

# 13

## SUDDEN DEATH

The three riders set off down the steep grade, unaware that they were being watched from the upper trail. Once he was out of sight, Ramsey had dismounted and taken up a position to study their next move. He had no intention of being denied what he now considered was his due. The one problem to securing the loot was his unarmed status.

But that could easily be remedied once his marks had left the recent scene of battle in Pandora's Gorge. A close scrutiny of the site through a telescope brought a bitter smile to the robber's warped features.

Chase Farlow had failed to divest the dead trappers of their weapons.

'You've made a big mistake there, old

buddy,' Ramsey muttered to himself. 'And I'm gonna see that you regret it.'

He waited for the riders and their fully laden mules to disappear before venturing out into the open and making his way back to the Gorge. A couple of buzzards were pecking at one of the corpses. Angry squawks were aimed at the intruder. But they flapped away at his approach, settling on a nearby pine branch.

Ramsey's wary eye scanned the immediate vicinity to ascertain that the other trappers were nowhere around. Thankful to be alone, he quickly frisked the bodies. It was clear that these dudes had not managed to secure any of the latest hardware. The choice of weaponry was decidedly limited. Old cap-and-ball revolvers together with single shot breech loading rifles were all he was able to appropriate. The most serviceable weapons were selected together with an ample supply of ammunition. They would have to suffice.

He did not linger in the Gorge. The

noxious smell of death hung over the battleground as he started down the trail bound for Coal Bank Pass. Giving Ramsey ample time to depart, the winged predators then resumed their interrupted feast.

The trail down to the Pass was clear enough. Ramsey reckoned that he was an hour behind the group. Chase would be the one to watch. The tracker knew he would have to be extra vigilant to ensure the crafty weasel was given no hint he was being followed.

That night was uncomfortable for the lone pursuer. He could see the welcoming presence of a campfire down below in a glade beside the thrashing waters of a mountain creek. But Ramsey had to make do with a cold camp to avoid being spotted. He gave thanks to the foresight of commandeering a bearskin coat worn by one of the dead trappers. It stunk to high heaven. But at least it kept him warm during the chill hours of darkness.

He assumed that Strawtop and the

girl would stay on at the Speinkampf place if'n the kid was adamant about what he had announced. A mean curse rumbled in Ramsey's throat. That double-dealer had a lot to answer for. But it was the gold Buck Ramsey wanted. Revenge was sweet, but it didn't buy you a life on easy street.

Once Chase had left them at the farm he would be on his own. A lone escort with only a horse and two mules for company until he delivered the gold to the smelter in Durango. A mirthless smile cracked Ramsey's tense features. Between the Pass and the town, there would be ample opportunity to catch his old sidekick out. And this time he would not be denied.

A hand strayed to the rust-caked .44 calibre Remington on his hip. It was a large, ungainly weapon, but effective. Ramsey had once met Buffalo Bill Cody while he was still working for the army. The legendary hunter claimed the revolver had 'never once let me down'. That was endorsement enough for

Ramsey. Deep down, he still hoped that the gun would not be fired in anger. All Ramsey wanted was to deter his old partner from any foolhardy attempt at retaliation.

★  ★  ★

The tracker paused on a ledge over-looking the Speinkampf homestead nestling in the valley below. It was the following day. Crops could be seen in fields surrounding the main buildings. It certainly looked to be a prosperous enterprise. Ramsey's gaze focused on the three riders as they approached the farm. His intention was to remain up here until such time as Chase left to continue his journey south, down the Animas Valley to Durango.

Meanwhile down below in the valley, Della was pointing to the small burial plot over to one side. Jacob Speinkampf was on his knees. His head was resting on the wooden cross at the head of his wife's grave. They paused for a moment, surveying the tragic scene.

However, Della was mystified. She was glad to be back following her traumatic experience in Hesperus. But a niggling sense that all was not right caused her to hold back. It was the middle of the day. Her father usually only visited the grave in the evening once the chores had been completed.

Chase picked up on the girl's hesitancy.

'Something wrong, Della?' he asked, pulling up alongside her.

The girl frowned. She did not answer as she ardently studied her motionless parent. And where was old T-Bone? The place appeared to be deserted. Yes, something was definitely not as it should be.

Before she could give voice to her concerns, a stumbling figure lurched into view from around the far right side of the house. It was T-Bone. And he was clearly in trouble. A flapping arm was raised in the air.

'Don't come any closer!' the old guy

shouted. The gravelly voice was cracked and rasping. Blood was clearly visible soaking through his shirt front. 'We've been attacked,' he gasped. 'They shot your pa, then . . . ' He never got to finish the sentence.

The deep-throated roar of a long gun erupted from the upper storey of the barn. Smoke emerged from the open window. A gurgled cry issued from the prospector's mouth as he went down. Desperately he tried to raise himself, but a second bullet finished him off.

Other bullets were then directed at the newcomers. But for the moment, luck was on their side. Della's hesitance kept them beyond an effective killing limit. Only the most expert of marksmen could bring somebody down at this range.

Chase immediately took control.

'Take cover,' he yelled, as bits of wood were chewed from a nearby gate post. These guys would soon find their range. And the only cover available was a wooden box full of old saddle tack and some hay bales. More bullets kicked sand up close to the scampering arrivals as they hurried across to the meagre protection.

Strawtop ushered Della over to the box where they plumped down. But Chase was not so lucky. By ensuring the other two were safe, he had left himself unduly exposed. A slug plucked at his sleeve. These guys were no greenhorn gunslingers. Another shell slammed into his thigh. He fell to the ground. Lying in the open he was a sitting target.

A raucous guffawing broke out from the barn.

'How's it feel to be on the receiving end, suckers?' More rabid hallooing followed the snide baiting. 'And this time, we aim to finish the job once and for all. And that gold you're toting can be our pay-out.'

Chase recognized the gravelly tones of Wolf Maggrie. His craggy features twisted in pain as he hugged the hard ground. But there was nothing he could do to rectify the matter. Was this to be his final sunset? Shot down by no-account riff-raff? A wave of nausea swept over him as another belt of agony ripped through his leg.

'I'm going out there to bring him back here,' Strawtop declared firmly. 'He's a goner for sure stuck in the open.'

Della gripped his arm, a worried frown creasing her silky features. It was without doubt a dangerous undertaking, but the kid was adamant.

He handed his rifle to her. 'Just point the barrel over towards the barn, and keep levering and firing until the slide clicks on empty. It's fully loaded with fifteen shells. Keep the butt well into your shoulder. It don't matter none if'n you miss. This repeater should keep their heads down until I can rescue him.' He looked to the girl for her understanding.

Although she had never fired a gun in her life, Della was no prissy missy. Having been brought up on a remote homestead had instilled a tough resilience that now came to the fore.

'Don't worry about me,' she insisted, resting the Winchester on the lip of the box. 'I've seen plenty of these things in action so you'll be kept well covered. Now get going.'

Gabe zig-zagged across to where Chase was lying.

A man had emerged from the barn. Gabe stared in astonishment. He was dismayed to see that he was a trapper. He remembered the ugly face from the hostile crowd at Hesperus, not to mention the recent gun fight of Pandora's Gorge. How had those critters managed to get down here before them? Maybe they were the skunks who had been robbing the pack trains coming out of Silverton.

He was given no time to speculate on these notions. The men in the barn began firing at him. Stuck in the open with his wounded partner was a flagrant invitation to meet the Grim Reaper. Strawtop was loath to establish an acquaintance yet awhile. He dropped to the side of Farlow, who was trying desperately to get his own six-shooter into action, but with little success. Bullets thudded into the ground beside them both, kicking dust into their faces.

'This sure is a pretty pickle we're in, boy,' croaked the wounded man, offering a wan smile. His face had turned a dull shade of grey. Gabe Strawtop was not amused. He lifted his own gun and returned fire. His shots clipped the edge of the barn, driving them back inside. Another bullet zipped past his ear. It had come from the small graveyard. One of the varmints must be over there. Only a matter of seconds remained before the killers finished the job they had started.

The notion flashed through Gabe's troubled mind that the trappers must have been privy to a short cut through the mountains. The meandering trail they had taken followed an easy gradient specifically engineered for pack mules. But it was longer.

His supposition was correct.

Once the Maggries and their associates had left Pandora's Gorge, luck had smiled on them. The horses had not strayed far. It was Danny who suggested they make use of the old Ute trail. He had used it to reach the trading post at Hermosa while courting Della Speinkampf.

'It's steep and needs care in descent but will save us a full day,' he emphasized. 'That way we can reach the farm ahead of those critters.'

Silas responded with a manic chuckle. 'That's a right good plan, little brother. They'll get the shock of their lives finding us a-waiting on them.'

Wolf was likewise impressed. 'You guys in with us?' he inquired of the other three men.

Wolf towered over them. His grim expression spoke volumes as to their fate should the answer not be to his liking.

The one called Punk Crystal looked at his buddy. Green River Dick Slater was a hump-backed skinner. It was he who helped organize the annual rendez-vous. The pair had only joined the pursuit because the Maggries owed them money for preparing a heap of beaver pelts for shipment. Danny intimated that the money would only be forthcoming if they helped bring back the woman. The Maggries' reputation in the camp as hard-nosed jaspers who never accepted no for an answer encouraged them to agree to the proposal.

Wolf smiled. The feral leer had more in keeping with a hungry bear than a human being. He now turned to the third man. Foxy Overdo was more circumspect. He owed Silas money, borrowed to purchase a new Stetson hat from a catalogue. It mattered little now that the treasured possession was lying at the bottom of the gorge. He had no option but to agree to the proposal. The only other survivor of the gun battle had returned to Hermosa for treatment to a shoulder wound.

On reaching the farm, Danny displayed no hesitation in shooting down Jacob Speinkampf when the sodbuster challenged them. Della had poured out her heart to him on the night before the wedding. This Bible-bashing turkey had struck his betrothed and poured scorn on her intention to marry a Hesperus trapper.

While ransacking the farmhouse, the intruders had almost been caught napping when old T-Bone Craddock had burst in through the door.

The new farm hand had been mending some harnesses in the barn when he heard the gunshot. It could only mean trouble. Jacob only had one rifle on the farm for shooting wild varmints and hunting deer for the cooking pot. An ancient single shot Hawken, it was always kept securely locked away.

Unless he had been careless in cleaning the weapon, that shot heralded trouble of the human kind. Without thinking, T-Bone sought out the gunny sack he kept in his own quarters where, unbeknown to his boss, a percussion .36 Navy Colt was kept hidden. The hand gun was well maintained, and always loaded and ready for action. Cocking the trigger, he hurried across to the main house and burst in through the door.

The intruders had upended the furniture and were scattering goods all over the place in search of plunder. The sudden appearance of T-Bone caught them by surprise. He immediately recognized Silas Maggrie. The bandage round his head confirmed his suspicion.

'You're the skunk who tried to bushwhack me down the Animas.' Without bothering to take aim, his pistol roared, spitting out a tongue of black powder and lead. The first shot went wide smashing a mirror on the wall.

Silas yelped. He had no desire for more injuries. Sheer panic caused him to drop down out of sight. The second bullet was more accurate, striking Foxy

Overdo in the throat. He was dead before his body hit the hard-packed floor.

Wolf and Danny quickly recovered their wits. Both men let fly with their pistols at the same time. T-Bone was slammed back against the wall. He slumped over and lay still. Nobody bothered to check his condition. The sudden eruption of terminal violence had shredded their tightly strung nerves.

'Better get set up,' Wolf ordered his associates. 'Those other critters could be here soon and we need to be ready to greet them.'

It was Danny who had the bright idea of draping the body of the dead farmer over the cross in his personal cemetery. Della had told him about her father's regular visits to the sacred enclosure. He had silently scoffed at such a weak-kneed antic. But now it would provide them with a welcome piece of realism that everything on the farm was hunky-dory.

'They'll see him there and figure it's safe to come right in. Then we'll have the rats firmly in our grip,' said Danny. The other brothers chuckled. Crystal and Slater joined in with rather less enthusiasm. Both were sweating copiously. And it was not due to any heat radiating from the late afternoon sun. This expedition they had joined had become much more serious than they had anticipated. But it was too late to pull out now.

Wolf and Silas settled themselves in the upper floor of the barn where two open windows looked out on to the front corral. Danny soon joined them. This was where their quarry would arrive. Punk was ordered to take up his position by the double doors below.

'You join the dead man over in the graveyard,' Wolf told Green River Dick. 'You'll have a perfect shot from there to catch them off guard.' It was a good strategy. Slater nodded then hurried across to the macabre site.

They did not have long to wait. An

hour later, the small group of riders could be seen approaching the outer gate.

'All set, boys,' announced Wolf, a lurid grin revealing broken and yellowed teeth. 'Let them come right into the corral. Then we'll give them a Maggrie welcome.'

It was Danny who realized that somebody was missing from the group out there.

'Where's that big dude with the black moustache?' he posited.

No opportunity for speculation was given as T-Bone Craddock suddenly appeared from the farm house, calling out a warning.

# 14

## BUCK SEES THE LIGHT

The first shots echoing up from the valley below bounced off the surrounding rocks. It sounded like an invasion force. Buck Ramsey's thought flashed back to the grim conflict of the War. Puffs of smoke issued from the barn. He was shocked into a momentary stupor. Within seconds, a full-blown battle had erupted down there. But old habits die hard. His army training was still firmly ingrained deep within the root of his being.

Without any thought for his own welfare, Ramsey knew where his obligation lay. The gold was forgotten. Chase was in desperate straits and needed his help. What had he been thinking anyway? Planning to rob his oldest friend was the action of a cowardly braggart. He must have been mesmerized by the Devil himself to even consider such a heinous caper.

Spurs dug into the appaloosa, urging the stallion down the acclivitous slope. The animal immediately leapt forwards. Ignoring all the potential hazards of a hasty descent, man and beast slithered and stumbled down the loose trail. Stones were dislodged. Tree roots endeavoured to bring the frenetic charge to a perilous halt. Luck more than skill enabled the horse to gain the lower ground without mishap.

Ramsey then urged the animal to a leg-stretching gallop. Knees tightly gripped Dancer's flanks, enabling the rider to palm a revolver in either hand.

'Chaaarrrrrrggge!' he hollered, the excitement of battle overcoming any sense of fear. Once again, it felt like he was in the midst of comrades at the Battle of Gettysburg.

Veering to one side, he chose to come upon the farm from the side where there was a blind spot affording protection from the bushwhackers inside the barn. Only in the nick of time did he notice the single gunman hiding in the small graveyard.

The frantic plunge from above had been achieved in record time.

Without thought for his own safety, Ramsey leathered the cayuse to an ever greater stride as he hurtled across the flat ground. So intent was the gunman in trying to finish off the two exposed men in the corral, he failed to heed Ramsey's sudden intervention. Dragging Dancer to a jostling halt, he quickly took aim and pumped three shots at the startled figure hiding in the hallowed ground.

Caught unawares, Green River Dick stood no chance. He pitched over on to his face. Satisfied that Slater would not be rising from the dead, the newcomer then ran across to where Strawtop was struggling to help the injured Chase Farlow to his feet. He pumped a couple of shots at the barn to show he meant business. Two heads quickly disappeared from view.

'Where in thunderation did you spring from?' exclaimed the stunned kid.

'Just get him back under cover while I keep these jaspers busy,' replied Ramsey curtly as he aimed and fired his pistols until they clicked on empty. This was no time for explanations. Della ably backed up the awkward man-handling with the Winchester.

As fast as was humanly possible under the circumstances, they backed off. Lady Luck was with them. Without sustaining any further injuries, they somehow managed to struggle back into the relative safety of the hay bales and tack box. Bullets from the trappers' guns plucked and fizzed all around. It was fortunate that their assailants were not armed with the latest Colts and Winchesters, otherwise the result would have been far more lethal.

By the time she was down to the last shell in the Winchester's magazine, Della had found her range. The final bullet from the carbine struck Punk Slater, who had made the mistake of exposing himself to obtain a better shot. He went down in the open door of the barn. Only the three Maggries were now left to continue the fight. Wolf cursed. The unexpected interference of that other dude had stymied their plans.

Huddled behind the bales, Chase was wheezing and gasping for breath. Although his injuries were not life-threatening, the wounds in his arm and leg were leaking too much blood. He knew they were safe for the moment. Nevertheless their situation was grim. Stuck out here behind limited cover with no water and dwindling ammunition, it could only be a matter of time before their assailants could pick them off one at a time.

But he still managed a smile for his old buddy. 'What took you so long getting here? I was beginning to think you'd lost your way and fallen down a ravine.'

'Glad to see that you ain't lost that sense of humour, old man,' Ramsey countered, matching his pal's grin with a raise of the eyebrows. 'Seems to me like you're gonna need it.'

'Can't disagree with you there, Buck.' Chase levered himself up on to one elbow. The banter was just like old times. And it felt good. But not so the tight spot in which they were now trapped.

A croaking voice managed to enunciate the grim facts. 'Looks like you've gotten yourself into a stalemate, pard. I sure am glad to see you, though.' Chase paused to draw breath. A gurgling jar rumbled up from his throat. His tongue was like a strip of dried leather. And they had no water. 'But we can't stay here. We'll have to take the fight to them.'

'And how do you propose we do that?'

Ramsey's sceptical inquiry intimated that he had acted on instinct after deciding to get involved in the scuffle.

He was aching all over. Age was fast catching up now the initial euphoria had abruptly dissipated. Stuck here with two empty hand guns did not augur well. An old Springfield was stuck in the saddle boot of his horse. But the appaloosa had wandered away, scared off by the gunfire.

'I'm plum out of ammo for these Remingtons, and that Winchester carbine is only useful as a club now.'

'My belt is still half full of .45 shells,' Strawtop interjected, eager to add his bit to the conflab. 'We can share them out.'

'I was thinking that we could challenge them,' suggested Chase. 'Make it a straight gunfight, us two agin those three. They're stuck in the barn with no place to go, just like us. What d'you reckon?'

Ramsey considered the idea. A beaming grin broke across his face. The black moustache twitched. 'I like it. Takes me back to that time in Sedalia when we took on Bulldog Bentley and his crew. We walked away then with nary a spilt drop of blood between us. No reason we can't achieve the same result here. Only problem is, buddy, you ain't up to it.'

'It's only my leg,' Chase protested. 'And the bullet has gone right through. Strap it up tight with the rifle acting as a splint and I'll be able to stand. I won't need to walk far. And it's only the left arm that's been shaved. Reckon my gun hand can still do its duty.'

'What about me, you guys?' Strawtop pressed. 'Why can't I join you?'

The older men shook their heads.

'Your job is to protect Della,' Ramsey declared for them both. 'This is where your future lies, Gabe. And this showdown was meant to be just for us two old dudes. It's written on the wind. Ain't that the truth, Chase?'

The ex-lawman nodded. 'He's right, boy. This ain't your fight anymore. It's between us and them.'

He was already fixing the rifle in position. With Della's help and three bandanas, it now supported his injured leg. Once Chase was satisfied he returned Buck's Colt Frontier and the two friends loaded up with shells from Strawtop's belt.

'If'n this don't go according to your plan, I'll carry it on from here,' the young man stressed, loading up his own gun in readiness.

'I wouldn't expect anything less from you, partner,' Ramsey commended his associate. Then he turned to address those waiting in the barn. 'Got a proposition for you guys,' he called out.

'What can you give us that we can't take for ourselves?' replied Wolf.

'This is a stand-off. And the longer it goes on, the more chance there is of some traveller passing by. Remember this farm is near the main trail to Durango.'

'He's right,' Danny hissed in his brother's ear. 'Our plan was to grab the girl and the gold, then head back to Hesperus. Now we're stuck in this barn.'

Wolf cursed. But he knew that what the kid said held water. 'So what do you have in mind?' he called back.

'A gunfight out in the open. Two of us versus you three. That's gives you the advantage,' replied Ramsey. 'My partner is wounded. But we're prepared to take our chances. The question is . . . have you Maggries gotten the nerve to take us on? Or are you just a bunch of yellow rats with no backbone?' He winked at Chase, knowing that the jibe would hit the mark. The gauntlet had been thrown down. Maintaining family pride would ensure that the Maggries accepted the challenge.

Wolf's rabid howl of anger was answer enough. 'We agree. But tell the other jasper to throw out his guns. We don't want no double-crosser spoiling our aim.'

'Do as he says, Gabe,' Ramsey ordered. The kid protested, but complied, knowing that there was no other way out.

'Holster your weapons and come on

out then. Soon as we're all in the open, it's every man for himself,' Ramsey called back.

Slowly the two sets of protagonists sidled out into the open, hands stretched out away from their holstered revolvers. Ramsey helped his buddy up and together they stepped forwards to meet their destiny.

'All for one' — whispered Ramsey.

— 'and one for all,' Chase finished, fixing his partner with a determined look. 'Just like old times.' Then side by side they walked out into the middle of the corral.

Chase's limp brought a sneer of derision from Silas Maggrie. 'You old dudes will soon be joining grey-beard over yonder.' A twitch of the head indicated the crumpled form of T-Bone Craddock.

It was Danny Maggrie who brought the proceedings to a brutal onset when he sneered out a rasping insult to the concealed Strawtop. 'Too yeller to match us, greenhorn?' he sniped.

'Guess all you're fit for is hiding behind a woman's skirt.'

That insult was one step too far for Gabe Strawtop. A howl of anguish roared out as he jumped to his feet and dashed out into the open, oblivious to the danger. Della screamed. But her tormented wail was lost amidst the sudden eruption of gunfire.

Strawtop grabbed up his Colt.45 and began unloading the bullets. His sole target was Danny Maggrie. Heedless for his own safety, he steadily pushed forwards, cocking and unleashing the death-dealing lead poison. His third shot found its mark. Danny went down on to one knee. Gabe did not falter. Advancing purposefully across the open ward, it was his last bullet that finished the job.

But the uncaring attitude had its price. A bullet from Silas Maggrie stopped him in his tracks. He spun round and fell to the ground. Della ran out and threw herself down next to his fallen body.

'Gabe, Gabe!' she wailed. 'Speak to me!'

A gurgled grunt brought a sigh of relief as the kid slowly opened his eyes. 'You can't get rid of me that easy,' he croaked before losing consciousness.

The remaining protagonists on either side stood their ground, pouring lead at one another. Smoke from the hot gun barrels twisted and writhed in the low breeze.

Wolf cried out with glee as one of his shots took Chase Farlow in the chest. The big man faltered but kept going. He leaned on the Winchester with his left hand still cocking and firing the Colt in his right. Before he went down, a smile of satisfaction creased the pain-ravaged face as Silas Maggrie fell to the ground.

Only Wolf and Buck Ramsey now remained on their feet. Buck shucked his empty revolver and snatched up the gun dropped by Chase. A quick check revealed there were still two shells left in the chambers. Advancing purposefully through the swirling tendrils of gun smoke, he saw the hesitant figure no more than ten paces ahead. Without thought, he emptied the revolver into the trapper.

Wolf coughed, his body arching under the impact of the lead slugs. Then he went down. The battle was over. But the ear-splitting thunder of gunfire lingered in the static air. Ramsey breathed deep, his gun arm hanging by his side. They had come through it. Yet how sweet was victory?

A pounding heart informed him in no uncertain terms that he was far too old for this sort of shindy. Gabe and Chase were both seriously wounded, old T-Bone Craddock and the farmer, dead. Only he, Buck Ramsey had come through unscathed. He felt guilty at having survived the deadly confrontation.

His first thought now was for his buddy. He hurried over to where Chase was lying. His friend was still breathing, but the wound in his chest left Ramsey in no doubt that it was a fatal injury. Chase was dying, and fully cognizant that his time on this earth was severely limited.

'Gee, old buddy. Has it come to this?' Tears bubbled from Ramsey's eyes. 'I was a greedy fool to even consider robbing you. That's a cross I'll have to bear for the rest of my days.' His head hung down in abject shame. 'Can you ever forgive me?'

Chase forced a tired smile, his glassy eyes flickering as life inexorably faded away. But he still managed a spirited reply.

'You just lost your direction for a spell, old-timer . . . Happens to us all at some point . . . Main thing is you came through good . . . in the end. Once you've delivered the gold to the Durango smelter and Will Bonney's paid you and Gabe off, could you do me one more favour?'

'You don't need to ask,' Ramsey sobbed. 'Anything that's in my power, you've got it.'

'Head back to Quemado and salvage my reputation. I know you can do it.' A spasm of pain lanced through the shattered frame. Chase paused until it eased before continuing. 'Remember what I told you about Stanton and him being in debt to Brett Sinclair?' Ramsey nodded. 'That's the key. You'll need to work out a plan.' Another stab of agony twisted his rapidly failing senses. Somehow, he managed to rally his thoughts one last time. 'I'll go to my grave happy . . . knowing that the name of Chase Farlow . . . is still respected . . . '

A trembling seizure wracked the tormented body. Rheumy eyes closed as the balance was inexorably tipped in favour of the scythe man. The sun had finally come down over the Sierras for the wrongly vilified former law officer.

Now it was up to Buck Ramsey to reverse matters.

# 15

## A PROMISE EXACTED

It was some weeks later that a dust-caked rider entered the main street of Quemado in New Mexico territory. Buck Ramsey had carried out the first of his deceased friend's final requests to the letter. The strong boxes had been delivered to the smelter at Durango and the money deposited in the bank. In so doing he had retrieved his self-respect, plus a substantial bonus from a delighted Will Bonney.

After hearing about the bizarre chain of events that had led to Chase Farlow's demise, the assay agent had immediately offered Buck his old pal's job. Buck had readily accepted. But there was one last thing that needed to be done before he could take up the appointment. Bonney did not stand in his way.

Heading south down the Animas Valley, he had called at the Speinkampf farm to deliver Gabe Strawtop's dues. The kid was recovering well under Della's careful supervision. He paused momentarily to say a few words in the small graveyard where Chase had been interred alongside the Speinkampfs. T-Bone Craddock had also found his final resting place. The small cemetery was becoming a mite crowded.

It was a thoroughly chastened Buck Ramsey who left the farm on his mission of resurrection, and retribution.

Gabe was all for accompanying him to Quemado. But it was obvious that the kid was not yet fit enough for such an arduous journey.

Buck hauled up outside the Fairplay saloon. According to Chase, this was the one owned by Brett Sinclair, the guy who was hopefully going to help him kick Mayor Stanton up the butt. Dismounting, he peered about. Nobody paid the scruffy drifter a second glance.

The thick moustache acted as an effective disguise for those citizens who had previously known him. He had also aged rather more than he liked since his brief spell as deputy to Chase Farlow. Arriving incognito was just how he wanted it. He stepped inside the saloon.

A lawman was standing at the bar. This must be Tate Hogan, the mayor's nephew.

'Another drink, marshal?' inquired a bartender. Buck suppressed a scowl. So the guy had indeed been promoted at Chase's expense. Without replying, the cocksure star packer grabbed a full bottle and without paying, hustled out of the saloon. None of the bar staff objected.

After taking a sip of his own beer, Buck called the barman over. 'Is Brett Sinclair available?' he asked.

'Who wants to know?' replied the suspicious barkeep, eyeing up the newcomer's trail-weary appearance. 'The boss only sees people by appointment.'

'He'll want to see me,' rasped Buck, irritated by the guy's surly attitude. He leaned across the bar to emphasize a cutting postscript. 'And if'n he learns that a feller has been turned away who can do him a big service, that turkey sure ain't gonna be very popular. Get my drift?'

It appeared that Smiler Redcap had indeed received the message loud and clear. But a gloomy expression remained pasted across the rubicund features as he hustled over to a door behind the bar. He knocked twice. A muted voice beyond found him entering the inner sanctum of the saloon boss.

Buck turned around. Drinking his beer, he purposefully surveyed the room while he waited. One or two faces were familiar. But nobody eyeballed the one-time deputy.

A minute later and Redcap signalled for Buck to come over. This time he was much more obsequious, bowing as he ushered the stranger into the presence of his employer. Brett Sinclair rose from behind a large desk. A hand stretched out to greet the newcomer. Buck accepted the proffered appendage. It was firm and welcoming.

Sinclair gave no indication that he was offended by the unkempt appearance of his visitor, even though the two were as disparate as chalk and cheese. The saloon boss was clad in a smart black suit. The cravat gracing his neck was adorned with a large diamond stickpin. He was clearly a man of substance.

Crystal clear blue eyes twinkled, revealing a hint of humour beneath the poker-faced façade. But Buck sensed that anybody who crossed this guy would live to regret their foolhardy actions.

'So what can I do for you, Mr . . . ?'

'The name is Buck Ramsey.'

Sinclair's face remained devoid of enlightenment. The name meant nothing to him. And why should it? Buck had been a deputy in Quemado before his time. He quickly perceived that small talk was not on this guy's agenda. So without any preamble, he went on to explain his presence.

The gambler listened intently. He said nothing as the bleak events unfolded. The lively eyes assumed a cold hardness. Sinclair was visibly shocked to learn of his old friend's violent demise. 'I always reckoned that Chase had been forced out by that conniving toad, Abner Stanton. But he left town before I could lend my support. That's the last I heard of him until now.'

Sinclair paced the room, hands clasped behind his back. A stern expression had replaced the deadpan demeanour. There was much to think on, following the lucid yet concise outline of Chase Farlow's subsequent career since being so ignominiously forced out of office. Buck allowed the listener to fully assimilate the facts without interrupting.

A long minute passed before the

gambler stopped. 'So let's get this straight. You want my help to turn the tables on Stanton and force him to acknowledge that Chase was badly treated?'

'That's about the heart of it,' Buck attested. 'Even in death, Chase Farlow deserves to have his reputation reinstated. Shooting down the Stanton kid was pure bad luck. After cleaning up the town and making it safe for everybody, he didn't deserve all the muck that was thrown at him.'

'I couldn't agree more,' Sinclair confirmed. 'Nothing would give me greater pleasure than to bring Stanton to his knees. The skunk has this town stitched up. His nephew has taken over as town marshal. And apart from Doc Watson, the rest of the council are in his pocket. So what do you have in mind, Buck?'

Buck's scheme to restore his old friend's standing had been formulated on the long trek south from Durango. By the time he reached Quemado, it had been honed to perfection. But would the gambler and saloon owner, known as Honest Brett Sinclair, agree to the devious chicanery involved in carrying it through successfully?

He was on tenterhooks as the highly respected businessman considered the proposition. His own reputation would be on the line if things went awry.

'You're asking a lot, Buck,' he declared pensively, following a reflective and somewhat brooding cogitation of the implications. 'The use of a marked deck to deliberately cheat is against all my principles. If'n it ever came to light, my own reputation for running an honest game would be in tatters. I'd be tarred and feathered and run out of town on a rail.'

'It's the only way to bring Stanton down,' Buck persisted. 'According to Chase, he has a weakness for the green baize that has found him in debt to you before. Chase reckons that's one of the reasons he was ousted from office so abruptly. Because the rat figured it would come to light and his control of the council would be finished.'

'We discussed it,' Sinclair concurred. 'But Chase would never have resorted to that sort of conduct. It was Stanton's warped sense of values that turned his head.'

'It will only be you and me that knows the truth of what's being played out,' insisted Buck, silently urging the gambler to give his backing to the plan. 'We can take the varmint for every penny he has, then force his hand to prevent the news of the humiliating fall from grace being made public.'

'What happens to the dough we take off'n him?' asked Sinclair.

Ramsey shrugged. Then a wry smile broke across his gnarled features. 'I'm sure there are plenty of good causes that would benefit from the big-hearted generosity of Honest Brett Sinclair.'

The gambler couldn't resist a jovial guffaw. 'The town sure does need a new schoolhouse. And Doc Watson has been trying to get funding for a hospital.'

And so the devious plot was put into action. The gambler had acquired numerous decks of marked cards over the years from tinhorns who had sought to infiltrate the various premises he had managed. The most skilfully engineered pack was selected for the forthcoming game.

Buck was instructed in their fraudulent conversion. An adept poker player himself, he was nevertheless completely hoodwinked by the amended cards until their imperfections were pointed out.

An invitation was sent out to Mayor Stanton that a no-limit poker game was to be held in the private quarters of Brett Sinclair that night. The gambler knew instinctively that the pompous official would not be able to resist the lure of a big game.

\* \* \*

'I would like you to meet Mayor Stanton, Mr Smith,' Sinclair said, introducing the stranger in town. Both men had felt it was circumspect for the newcomer to adopt an alias on the off-chance that Stanton would recall the name of Ramsey. The pair shook hands. Unlike that of Brett Sinclair, it was like handling a wet fish. And he was still the arrogant snob that Buck remembered.

During his last sojourn in Quemado, the skunk had never given him the time of day. A mere deputy was too low down in the pecking order as far as the mayor was concerned. In consequence, Buck had little fear of being recognized. The luxuriant facial hair helped, not to mention the smart suit and accessories borrowed from Brett Sinclair's extensive wardrobe. Luckily they were of a similar build.

'Will you be in town long, Mr Smith?' The mayor was patently impressed by a man's appearance.

'I'm looking for some good land investments,' purred the trickster, lighting up a cigar. 'Perhaps you could point me in the right direction.'

'As a man of influence in these parts, I am always ready to do business with a like-minded gent. Look me up tomorrow.'

Ramsey gave the offer a curt bow before turning to the fourth member of the syndicate. This guy was the oldest of the quartet. He knew straightaway that this was Doc Watson. With Ramsey's approval, Sinclair had taken the old guy into his confidence. Four people were needed for the game to be conducted along regular lines of play. Buck's smile was genuine. He knew that Chase would have fully approved of the old guy being included.

The medic had been made aware of the scam that was about to be enacted. Having only recently been voted off the town council, he was more than willing to witness the perpetrator of his expulsion receive his just deserts.

With glasses filled and cigars lit, the game commenced. Sinclair dealt the first cards. Only he and Buck were mindful of the tampered cards. It had been agreed between them initially to allow Stanton to win steadily. Only later was a losing streak to be enacted, and then with caution. Just enough wins to keep him from suspecting that a scam was being perpetrated with him as the patsy.

That was when the stakes would be raised. Doc would call it a day along with Sinclair. Ramsey wanted to be in at the kill. The moment when Stanton would assume he had a sure-fire, unbeatable hand. In no time the ante had been raised to a level that would effectively bankrupt the loser.

The final call was made after much sweat had been expended by the official. His face was purple with excitement as he made the final call. He laid down three aces and two kings — a full house. It could only be beaten by four of a kind. The odds against that happening were substantial. Certainly enough for Stanton to risk everything.

Sure he had won, Stanton made to

rake in the large mound of ten, twenty and fifty dollar bills. His eyes were on fire, his breath coming in short gasps of delight. Then a hand reached across the green baize and stayed his hand.

'Forgive me if'n I'm mistaken, Mr Mayor,' came the whispered announcement from Smith. 'But in poker, doesn't four threes beat your hand?' Slowly and deliberately to draw out the moment of truth, he purposefully laid the cards out, one by one.

Stanton's mouth dropped open. He couldn't believe what he was seeing.

'Th-that c-can't be right,' he stammered, the blood draining from his face. 'I was sure that . . . ' He was lost for words.

'The cards don't lie, Abner,' stated Doc Watson, struggling to keep the delight from his voice. 'You know that Brett always runs an honest game. Mr Smith has won, fair and square.'

Maintaining eye contact, Buck slowly raked the huge wad of cash over to his side of the table, including the IOU for two thousand dollars attested to and countersigned by Sinclair and the doctor. 'Perhaps you would be good enough to have the money ready for collection before I leave town in the morning,' he stated in a flat yet decisive tone. The brusque expectancy left the debtor in no doubt he meant to exact every last nickel from the loser.

'But I ain't got that much in the bank,' Stanton burbled. Panic as to the disgrace failure to honour the debt would bring was written across the ashen features.

'What you can't afford to lose, you shouldn't bet,' rasped Buck Ramsey, standing over the quaking lump. 'You have until tomorrow to pay, or else . . . ' He deliberately left the sentence unfinished. Stanton's terror-filled imagination could fill in the results of his ignominy.

Five minutes passed while the fallen official was left to contemplate the humiliation of being branded a charlatan. A mayor who failed to pay his debts was unworthy of office. He would have to sell up everything he had accrued over the years. The crushing abasement of destitution loomed large in his mind.

'There is one way for you to emerge from this hole with a measure of dignity,' declared the mysterious Mr Smith.

Stanton's eyes flickered. A lifeline had been offered. He had no idea what it entailed. But anything was better than the utter disgrace of being branded a penniless fraud. 'Anything,' he warbled. 'Whatever it is I'll do it.'

A lawyer had already prepared the certified document that Ramsey now produced from his inside pocket. No name had been appended in order that the lawyer was unaware of its significance. Sinclair took hold of the sealed paper and wrote the name of Abner Stanton in the space provided.

The list of stipulations was extensive. It included his immediate resignation as mayor, reduction of rents on all businesses, an immediate election in which all citizens of at least one year's residence could vote to elect council officials, including the mayor and town marshal.

But most significant for Stanton was the additional sworn statement exonerating Chase Farlow from blame, regarding the unfortunate shooting at Macy's gun store. By signing the declaration, he confirmed that the ex-lawman had only been carrying out his bounden duty at the time of the break-in. His actions were, therefore, wholly in keeping with those expected from a law officer.

The gambler pushed the document under the nose of the morose toad. 'Sign it. Then you can leave here taking the IOU with you.' He handed the ex-mayor a pen. Stanton scowled, trying to brazen it out.

'This was a set-up all along,' he blustered. 'You can't get away with it. Once the council know about your duplicity, it's you skunks who will be forced to leave Quemado, not me.'

Ramsey was done with playing the gentleman. He grabbed the odious turkey by the scruff of the neck and hauled him over the green baize table. Cards and money were scattered across the floor.

'Listen up, you overblown bag of wind.' The threatening growl instantly silenced Stanton's imprudent piece of bravado. 'Fail to sign and I'll string you up from the rafters and paddle your fat backside until you do. Chase Farlow was a better man than rats like you could ever be. It's down to your lowdown connivance that he's dead.'

He paused to allow this momentous disclosure to sink in. A tightening of his rough hold elicited a choking gurgle from the quivering lump of jelly.

'I gave him a promise before he passed on to clear his good name. If you figure I'm bluffing . . . these good men here will back my play to the hilt.'

Grim looks, cold as ice, from Honest

238

Brett Sinclair and Doc Watson, speared the braggart, assuring him that he would not be leaving that room until he agreed to their terms. The bluster dissipated like air from a punctured balloon. He realized that the game was up, in more ways than one. A brief nod and he took up the pen and scrawled his name on both documents.

Sinclair handed over the IOU. 'Now get out. And if'n I see your miserable hide in Quemado by this time tomorrow, expect trouble.' He left the substance of the implied threat unspoken. Abner Stanton had gotten the message loud and clear.

The disgraced man stumbled out of the room.

It was some minutes before the three men were able to breathe freely again. The successful outcome of their devious stunt had left all three somewhat jaded. It was Honest Brett who finally brought the proceedings back to a manageable level.

'I think this calls for a drink,

gentlemen.' He filled their glasses. 'A toast to the redeemed memory of Chase Farlow, a special lawman impossible to replace.'

'CHASE FARLOW!!'

We do hope that you have enjoyed reading this large print book.

Did you know that all of our titles are available for purchase?

We publish a wide range of high quality large print books including:
**Romances, Mysteries, Classics**
**General Fiction**
**Non Fiction and Westerns**

Special interest titles available in large print are:
**The Little Oxford Dictionary**
**Music Book, Song Book**
**Hymn Book, Service Book**

Also available from us courtesy of Oxford University Press:
**Young Readers' Dictionary**
**(large print edition)**
**Young Readers' Thesaurus**
**(large print edition)**

For further information or a free brochure, please contact us at:
**Ulverscroft Large Print Books Ltd.,**
**The Green, Bradgate Road, Anstey,**
**Leicester, LE7 7FU, England.**
**Tel:** (00 44) **0116 236 4325**
**Fax:** (00 44) **0116 234 0205**

## REINS OF SATAN

## Lee Clinton

*The reins of Satan are harnessed to the sins of violence* . . . Civil War veteran Gabe McDermott has spent the last thirty years working as an enforcer for anyone who can pay. Desiring to escape his past and settle down, he turns in his young partner Hiram Miller for a $1,500 reward. However, when Hiram is hanged without a trial, the execution awakens Gabe's lost conscience. Memories from his former life return to haunt him, and his nerve fails — just when Satan decides to call . . .